Marcia Muller created the contemporary hardboiled woman detective with her first Sharon McCone novel, and this groundbreaking series is now over two decades old. Much-loved bestsellers, the McCone books have been translated into eight languages and there are two million copies in print worldwide. In 1993, Marcia Muller received the Private Eye Writers of America Life Achievement Award. Marcia Muller lives in northern California.

MARCIA MULLER
LISTEN TO THE SILENCE
A SHARON McCONE MYSTERY

Published in Great Britain by The Women's Press Ltd, 2000
A member of the Namara Group
34 Great Sutton Street, London EC1V 0LQ
www.the-womens-press.com

First published in the United States of America by Warner Books, Inc,
2000

This book is a work of fiction. Names, characters, places and
incidents are the product of the author's imagination or are used
fictitiously. Any resemblance to actual events, locales, or persons,
living or dead, is coincidental.

British Library Cataloguing-in-Publication Data
A catalogue record for this book is available from the British Library.

ISBN 0 7043 4672 9

Printed and bound in Great Britain by Cox & Wyman Ltd,
Reading, Berkshire

For Cathy Pronzini and Jim Moen
(Csoda and Kiro too!)

Many thanks to

Josie Bennington, for lending her airplane to McCone and Ripinsky.

Maureen Harty, for information on Boise, Idaho.

Kathy McIntosh, for a great tour of that city.

Robin Reese, for the use of her first name and "the yarn people."

Lieutenant Jim Tibbs, for insights about the Boise Police Department.

The Usual Suspects—you know who you are!

And Bill, without whom . . .

LISTEN TO THE SILENCE

Saturday

·

SEPTEMBER 2

5:55 P.M.

The phone receiver began a series of staccato beeps. I stared as if it were a foreign object, then replaced it in the cradle. My world had tilted a few minutes ago, and everything seemed askew.

I went over to the windows and looked down at the lower deck of the Sea Cliff house where the post-wedding party was coming to an end. It was a perfect September day, warm and clear, without a wisp of fog to spoil the view of the Golden Gate—the start of the season we San Franciscans consider our summer. The guests were dressed in brightly colored clothing, ranging from shorts and Hawaiian shirts to formal attire. Typical eclectic crowd for a California wedding.

And it had been a terrific wedding. My friend and operative, Rae Kelleher, and my former brother-in-law, country music star Ricky Savage, exchanged vows by the deck rail, the Pacific gleaming in the background. Then the band struck up the title song of his new album, *Red*—written and recorded as his wedding surprise for Rae—and the serious partying got under way. Caterers passed through with gallons of champagne and mounds of shellfish, caviar, and hot hors d'ouevres; we ate and drank like pigs in heaven. The wedding cake—nontraditional chocolate—was decimated minutes after the bride and groom cut it. Even Ricky's six children by my sister Charlene, initially subdued by their father's remarriage, perked up and were soon behaving in the various modes that had earned them the nickname the Little Savages.

When it came time for Rae to change from her wedding gown to going-away clothes, I went inside with her to perform my final maid-of-honor duty—namely, to ensure she and Ricky didn't miss their honeymoon flight to Paris. The phone was ringing and she said, "Why don't you get that? I'm old enough to dress myself." So I left her and went to the living-room extension and picked up.

And my world changed.

Now I put a hand to my hair, touched the circlet of autumn flowers I wore. It was wilted. My dress, a silk swirl of similar shades, was rumpled, and I was barefoot because I'd been dancing. On the deck below, the band had stopped playing and people were starting to drift inside. Soon they'd be spilling up the stairway to watch the couple leave, and I'd need to be on hand and smiling as Rae tried to lob her bouquet at me.

"God, how can I?" I whispered.

Behind me I heard footsteps and voices. The room was filling up, but I stood frozen. I *had* to pull myself together, turn around.

You've been through lots worse, McCone. Just act as if nothing's happened. Pretend you never picked up that receiver; don't wreck Rae and Ricky's moment. Plenty of time to break the news later.

I squared my shoulders, took my own advice, faced the crowd. They were all talking and laughing, but the sound seemed curiously muted. I spotted Ricky's youngest child, Lisa, a gob of frosting on her cheek. My office manager, Ted Smalley, and his partner, Neal Osborn, looked handsome in vested suits and wild ties. Attorneys Anne-Marie Altman and Hank Zahn held hands with their adopted daughter, Habiba Hamid—proof that some families, no matter how oddly assorted, worked. And there was Hy Ripinsky, my very significant other. . . .

Hy was talking with Ricky's manager, Kurt Girdwood, and didn't notice me. Quickly I turned away, started walking toward the staircase Rae and Ricky would be coming down. I couldn't let Hy see me; he'd instantly know something was wrong. In the years we'd been together I'd never once been able to conceal my true feelings from him.

A tap on my shoulder. Mick Savage, Ricky's oldest son and best man, and my agency's computer expert. His blond hair was tousled and he had traces of bright red lipstick on his mouth. Charlotte Keim, the source of the lipstick and another of my operatives, clung to his arm.

Mick said, "Wedding came off okay, huh?"

I managed a grin. "Great. And neither of us lost the rings."

"What the hell's taking them so long?" He glanced at his watch, probably anxious to get out of there and back to the condo he and Keim had started sharing two weeks before.

"They're going to *Paris,* darlin'," she said. "Takes time to get gussied up for a trip like that."

"Hell, Dad's probably grabbed Rae for a quickie."

"Let's have a little decorum here," I told him. Not that the remark offended me; knowing the bridal couple, it might very well be accurate. But Mick expected an auntly rebuke and would have found it odd had he not received one.

Then Rae and Ricky came down the staircase. She was stunning in a blue suit, her long red-gold curls loose on her shoulders; his handsome face looked happier and more at peace than I'd ever seen it. He caught my eye, pointed to Rae's bouquet, and winked. I shook my head, made a fending-off gesture.

Raising his hands for quiet as he did on stage, he called, "Okay, folks. It's time for the next lucky couples to learn their fate! Gentlemen first—preferably single ones." As the men moved forward, he turned his back, waved Rae's lacy green garter in the air, and hurled it over his shoulder. It landed in the hands of Jerry Jackson, his drummer.

"Been there, done that!" Jerry yelled. But he pocketed the garter carefully and grinned at his pretty blond woman friend.

"Now it's the ladies' turn," Ricky announced, motioning for us to draw closer. When I didn't move, he looked at me and frowned; he was another man I had trouble deceiving. Quickly I stepped forward, and he shrugged: Sister Sharon, as he sometimes still called me, was simply being weird again. "Throw it, Red, so we can get out of here."

Rae pivoted and heaved the bouquet over her shoulder; she must've been on radar, because it flew straight at me. I sidestepped, and it ended up in Keim's arms.

"No way!" Charlotte exclaimed. "Rae may be the marryin' kind, but not *this* gal!" She tossed the flowers away, and Ricky's college-age daughter, Chris, caught them. She blushed, rolled her eyes, and smiled up at her date, a UC Berkeley wide receiver.

I let out a sigh, glad that this ordeal was nearly over. Catering people appeared with bags of confetti, and then Rae and Ricky ran the gauntlet to a waiting limo. As it drove off, more trays of champagne were circulated, but the party had a definite winding-down feel.

"McCone." Hy came up behind me, put his hands on my shoulders.

"Hey there." I rested my cheek against one of them. "Well, we got off scot-free in the garter-and-bouquet department, in spite of the happy couple's intentions."

"You sure that's a good thing?"

The question surprised me. "Since when have we needed legal sanction—" My voice broke, the strain overwhelming me.

For a moment Hy didn't speak, just tightened his grasp on my shoulders. Then he said softly, "I've been watching you. You've done a good job of fooling everybody but me. What's wrong?"

". . . Let's go down on the deck, and I'll tell you."

The sun had dipped below the Marin County headlands, and the temperature had dropped. The musicians were packing up their gear while the caterers moved about filling plastic bins with plates and silverware and glasses. I went to the rail and leaned there, staring at the slow-moving lights of a departing container ship.

Hy came up beside me. "If you're cold, you can have my jacket."

"I'm okay."

"Temperature-wise, maybe. Now, what's wrong?"

I turned toward him. Drew comfort from his sensitive dark eyes and the concerned lines of his hawknosed, mustached face. Felt, with a painful and unexpected jolt, how empty my life would be should I lose him.

He took my face between his hands, eyes gentle on mine, and waited.

"There was a phone call when Rae and I went inside," I finally said. "From my brother John. I've been keeping the news to myself because I didn't want to upset the kids and Ricky. Even after he and Charlene got divorced, he'd remained close—" I broke off, sucking in my breath.

"Something's happened to Charlene?"

I shook my head.

If you put it into words, it makes it real.

"Who, honey?"

Atypical term of endearment, for Hy.

"My father. He's . . . he's dead. He had a heart attack this afternoon. In the garage of the San Diego house, all alone, working on some carpentry project."

There, I've said it. Pa's dead. And in spite of all the death I've seen over the course of my career, I don't know how to deal with this.

Hy did, for the moment. He put his arms around me, pulled me close, and held me.

11:17 P.M.

"Can't sleep, McCone?"

"Uh-uh."

"Sure you don't want me to fly you down there in the morning?"

"No. A commercial flight's faster."

"At least let me come along. I should be there for the funeral."

"Didn't I tell you? There won't be one. Pa didn't believe in them. John's having him cremated, and on Monday the two of us will scatter him at sea."

"Just you and John? What about the others?"

"Charlene's at a conference in London. Patsy can't leave the new restaurant. John couldn't get hold of Joey—his phone's been disconnected."

"Well, if I went down with you, I could rent a plane and fly it while you and John scatter—"

"No, I'll do that. Besides, there's something else I need from you."

"Just ask."

"It's kind of a big thing. Would you mind the agency for me? Whenever I went away before, I put Rae in charge, but now—"

"No problem. I'm between projects, but even if I wasn't, I'm always here for you."

"I know."

But now I know that "always" is a lie.
Now I know that, in the end, death is the only certainty.

Monday

·

SEPTEMBER 4

3:21 P.M.

"I can't do this," my older brother John said.

I brought the rented Cessna level over the Pacific, pulled back on power till the engine made the distinctive purr that told me, without looking at the tachometer, that it was at the proper RPM for slow flight.

"What?"

"I said, I can't do this."

I glanced at him. A nervous flier under any circumstances, he hunched in the right seat, his arms wrapped around the plain cardboard box and metal urn on his lap. His blond hair flopped onto his forehead, and there were pronounced lines between his eyebrows and around his mouth. For all his forty-eight years, he resembled a miserable, scowly little boy.

"Why not?" I asked.

He shrugged, looked away.

Oh, God, he was exhibiting full-blown symptoms of the infamous family failing—the inability to properly deal with one's dead. It was the reason he held two containers of ashes, Pa's in the box, and our paternal grandfather's in the urn. The urn had lingered for twenty-some years on the top shelf of our father's coat closet, and yesterday I'd come down to San Diego determined that Grandpa would be scattered along with Pa. Now it seemed John was no more capable of this duty than our father.

I decided a matter-of-fact, unemotional approach was called for. "If you're worried about opening the window while we're in flight, it's no big deal. And you don't have to lean out. Just tip the container toward the plane's tail."

"Why the tail?"

"Because if you do it toward the nose, the prop wash'll blow the stuff back inside."

Wrong image to call up. John winced and closed his eyes, big hands protectively cradling the containers.

"They're not just 'stuff,' you know," he said.

"Sorry. I'm as unhappy about this as you, and I guess I don't want to think of what's in there as Pa and Grandpa."

He nodded in acceptance of my apology but didn't look at me. After a minute he asked, "Shar, are you sure this is what Pa wanted?"

"He put it in his will."

"But that will was made a while ago. Maybe he changed his mind."

"Then he'd've added a codicil. Pa was meticulous about details." Meticulous, except for the minor detail of his father's remains residing with the overcoats.

"Well, what about Grandpa? He wouldn't fly, ever. D'you really think he'd appreciate being hurled out of a plane?"

"Beats spending eternity on the shelf next to Pa's baseball caps."

"You're being pretty damn flippant for somebody who just lost her father!"

"And you're making a huge, painful production out of this! Just scatter them!"

He was silent again, clutching his precious cargo.

I could sympathize with his inability to perform this final rite; letting go had never been all that easy for me, either. And he'd been closer than any of us to Pa, particularly in these last few years. Still, somebody had to—

"For God's sake, hold the plane!" I exclaimed.

"Do *what*?"

"Put your feet on the rudders and your hand on the yoke and keep us level." I opened my window.

"What're you going to—"

"Feet on the rudders, like so." I pointed down at mine. Slowly John positioned his. "Now touch the yoke with your right hand—lightly, don't grip or yank on it. Just make little adjustments."

"I can't—"

"You've watched me do it. It's easy."

"I . . . okay." He made a few experimental moves.

"That's right. It pretty much flies itself. You're doing fine."

"Doing fine," he said doubtfully.

"Now give me one of them." I motioned at the containers while loosening my seat belt.

"Uh, who?"

"Grandpa. He's been waiting longer."

After a hesitation, he passed the urn to me. Looked straight ahead as I pried the lid off. I twisted in the seat, extended my arm through the window, and tipped the receptacle. Watched the ashes and bits of bone be borne away on the air currents.

James McCone, finally out of the closet.

I resisted an unseemly urge to giggle as I put the lid back on the urn and stuck it in the carrying space behind me.

John would be furious with me if I laughed at a time like this. He didn't share my offbeat and sometimes irreverent sense of humor, although I was fairly sure both Pa and Grandpa would have appreciated the absurdity of the situation.

Suddenly the plane's nose lurched upward and it started rolling violently from side to side. For some reason John had pulled back on the yoke, was now gripping it with both hands and trying to steer the aircraft like a car.

"Let go!" I yelled. "Get off the rudders!"

He hung on, grimacing. By the time I wrestled the controls from him, the stall horn was wailing.

"What the hell!" he shouted.

"It's okay. It's nothing." I controlled the stall with light, alternating pressure on the rudders, dropped the nose.

"Nothing?" he said weakly, wiping sweat from his pale face.

"Happens all the time to beginners." Thank God I'd gotten it in hand, though! The plummet that accompanies an uncontrolled stall was one experience I didn't want to treat him to—particularly on an occasion like this.

"I'm not beginning anything," he said. "My piloting minutes are at an end."

"Nonsense. You were doing great. Take over again."

"No way."

"It's that, or . . ." I motioned at the cardboard box.

He eased back onto the rudders, touched the yoke as if he feared it might burn him.

"Now give me Pa."

John's left hand grasped the box tightly; for a few seconds I was afraid he might refuse. Then, finally, his fingers loosened; they caressed it gently before he handed it to me.

I removed the lid. Hesitated, staring at the sea where Pa,

a sailor, had wanted to be laid to rest. Tears blurred my vision, and I felt a wrenching under my breastbone. Images flashed through my mind: nothing momentous, just small things.

Pa putting together a swing set on my sixth birthday. His ruddy face beaming when I rolled my first strike on a family bowling outing. His photographs of us, in which he always managed to cut off some essential body part. The impish gleam in his eyes as he sang the ribald folk ballads that he knew vexed my mother. The key chain with the inlaid wooden fob that he'd made and proudly presented to me when I bought my house.

It was a minute before I could hold the box out the window and let his ashes trail away.

When I turned back to John, I was surprised to find him flying with a sure hand. He smiled at me and said, "Thanks."

"You're welcome."

I let him pilot for a few minutes more. Before I took over and headed for land, he dipped the wings twice in tribute to Pa and Grandpa.

7:10 P.M.

I hung up the phone and heaved a huge sigh of relief. From across the family room of my father's house in San Diego's Mission Hills district John asked, "So how's Ma?"

"Sad. Subdued. But she still found plenty to bitch about."

"Let me guess: Why couldn't Pa have a funeral, like a normal person? Why aren't you staying with her and Melvin, instead of in this empty house? How come we're letting Nancy make off with all his worldly goods?"

"That, and more." I joined John on the ratty sofa, picked up my glass of wine from where he'd set it on the end table.

"So what'd you tell her?"

"That Pa wasn't a normal person, so he could hardly be laid to rest in a normal way. That I didn't want to stay up in Rancho Bernardo because I've got things to do here. That Nancy deserves whatever's left, for putting up with him." Nancy Sullivan was the woman Pa had more or less lived with the past few years—both at her La Jolla condo and on the road in his Airstream trailer. He seldom visited the Mission Hills house, except to putter in the garage workshop where he'd died.

"And Ma said?"

"After that I tuned her out."

"She does have one point: Why stay here? This house is pretty depressing, with most of the furniture gone. Where'd you sleep last night? On this couch?"

"Yes. It wasn't so bad." And I'd been able to indulge my grief in private.

"Well, tonight you should try out my new sofa bed."

"Can't. I want to get started sorting through the boxes in the garage, so I can go home Wednesday or Thursday. Last week I picked up a couple of important clients; I need to oversee the jobs."

"Hy can't do that?"

"He's not really an administrator." Hy was a partner in a corporate security firm, Renshaw & Kessell International. He specialized in hostage negotiation and other, more esoteric, skills.

John got up and went to the kitchen for another beer. When he came back, I studied our reflections in the darkened glass door to the backyard. We were so different: he, blond and big-boned and snub-nosed; I, dark and slender with chiseled features that were a genetic throwback to my Shoshone great-grandmother. I was the only one of the five of us who had inherited Mary McCone's Native American looks. No wonder I'd always felt like the odd duck in an already odd family.

"The thing about Nancy getting Pa's stuff," John said. "That's just Ma being sour-grapesy because he found somebody else after the divorce."

"Why? She found Melvin *before* they split." Melvin Hunt owned a chain of coin-operated laundries, and Ma had met him while patronizing one of his establishments when her washing machine broke down.

"I know, it's not logical, but Ma's not logical. Anyway, Charlene and Patsy already took the things they wanted when Pa moved in with Nancy. Joey doesn't care, and all I wanted were Pa's watch and service medals, which Nan gave me yesterday." We'd visited her in the evening, found her being well cared for by her grown daughter. "Is there anything in particular you'd like?"

I smiled wryly. "I've already got it—the dubious privilege of going through the stuff stored in the garage. Wonder why he specifically wanted *me* to handle that?"

"He said you were the only one with enough brains and patience for the task."

"Thank you, Pa—I think." I raised my glass and toasted the heavens.

9:15 P.M.

The garage was so crammed with boxes and bins and odds and ends of furniture that a car wouldn't fit—a manifestation of the pack-rat condition I'd come to think of as

McCone's Syndrome—and the cleared area by Pa's work-bench wasn't large enough to unpack things in. I went over there anyway, looked at the project he'd been work-ing on when he died. A small box constructed of finely milled samples of exotic woods; the pieces were all cut, and it was almost finished. I'd glue the rest in place, and it would be what I'd take away to remember him by.

First things first, though: the cartons. I carried several into the house and got started.

Miscellaneous clothing and uniforms from his days as a chief petty officer in the Navy. Those I would give to Good-will. Books, mostly adventure novels and thrillers. Donate to the library. More wood samples, broken and outdated tools, package upon package of corroded batteries, ammu-nition for guns he had no longer owned, half a dozen old cameras of the point-and-shoot variety, ancient packets of seeds and sacks of bulbs, hundreds of ballpoint pens, glue that had hardened in much-squeezed tubes, mason jars full of nails and screws, old road maps for damned near the entire United States and Canada, shelf brackets and hooks and braces, telephone cords and connectors, margarine tubs and lids—good God, hadn't he ever gotten rid of *anything*? And what the hell was I supposed to do with it all?

My eyes felt gritty and my head ached. I got up, fetched a couple more boxes from the garage, went to take some aspirin. Ten-fifty by the kitchen clock, and I'd scarcely made a dent in the accumulation. The contents of the next box would require careful sorting, too; it was labeled LEGAL PA-PERS.

Birth certificate, marriage certificate, divorce decree. Re-tirement papers from the Navy. Two old wills, pink slips on the Chevy Suburban and the Airstream trailer. Grant deed on the house to a corporation Charlene and Ricky had once formed; they'd bought it from him with the agreement he could live out his days here—their way of ensuring that he wouldn't have to sell it and move when he and Ma got divorced. Funny, I hadn't thought about what would happen to the house. I supposed Charlene had gotten it as part of her settlement with Ricky; she'd probably want to put it on the market.

The idea of the place being sold didn't bother me, as it once would have. It was no longer home in any sense. Home was the earthquake cottage I shared with two cats in San Francisco's Glen Park district. It was Hy's ranch in the high desert country near Tufa Lake. It was Touchstone, our joint property on the Mendocino Coast, where our dream house was rapidly nearing completion. Even my offices at Pier 24½ were more of a home than this empty shell of a place.

The thought of those offices reminded me of the two new clients and my need to get back to San Francisco. I dug into the papers with renewed vigor. Passport. Expired Navy ID card. Old bank and savings-account statements. PG&E stock certificate. Small whole-life policy with Ma still listed as beneficiary. A folder containing report cards: mine. Why the hell had he kept them? Photocopies of my high school and college diplomas. I didn't know he'd made them. U.S. Savings Stamps booklets in each of our names, none full. Folder with copies of our birth certificates and . . .

What was this?

Gerald A. Williams
1131 Broadway
San Diego, California
555-1290

Attorney for Petitioners

SUPERIOR COURT OF CALIFORNIA
COUNTY OF SAN DIEGO

In the matter of the	)	No. 21457
Petition of:	)	
	)	
ANDREW JOHN McCONE	)	
and	)	PETITION FOR
KATHRYN SYLVIA McCONE,	)	ADOPTION
	)	(Independent)
Adopting Parents.	)	
_____	)	

Petitioners allege:

1. The name by which the minor who is the subject of this petition was registered at birth is BABY GIRL SMITH.

2. The petitioners are husband and wife and reside in the County of San Diego, State of California, and desire to adopt BABY GIRL SMITH, the above-named minor child who was born in San Diego, California, on September 28, 1959. The petitioners are adult persons and more than ten years older than said minor.

3. The parents entitled to sole custody of the child have placed the child directly with the petitioners for adoption and are prepared to consent to the child's adoption by petitioners.

4. The child is a proper subject for adoption. The petitioners' home is suitable for the child and they are able to support and care properly for the child. The petitioners agree to treat the child in all respects as their own lawful child.

5. Each petitioner hereby consents to the adoption of the child by the other.

WHEREFORE, petitioners pray that the Court adjudge the adoption of the child by petitioners, declaring that each petitioner and the child thenceforth shall sustain toward each other the legal relation of parent and child, and have all the rights and be subject to all the duties of that relation; and that the child be known as SHARON ELIZABETH McCONE.

Dated: October 1, 1959.

Andrew John McCone

Kathryn L. McCone

Gerald K. Allen
Attorney for Petitioner

Shock washed over me like a flood of icy water. My hands started trembling as I gripped the photocopied document.

... desire to adopt BABY GIRL SMITH ...

... be known as SHARON ELIZABETH McCONE ...

Adopted?

"Mama, Joey says I'm not his sister!"

"Why? Why would he say a thing like that?"

"Because I don't look like him or John or the new baby."

"But you do look like your great-grandmother. Remember her?"

". . . No."

"Well, she was an Indian, a Shoshone. You inherited her looks."

"How come only me, and not the others?"

"That kind of thing just happens. It makes you special. Always remember that."

"Pa, why did John call me a throwback?"
"Because they're studying genetics in his science class. The way it works, we all have these little bits of matter called genes that get passed on from our ancestors. They determine what you look like. You're only one-eighth Indian, but you got more of your great-grandmother's genes than is usual. A person like you is a throwback to an earlier generation."
"Is that good or bad?"
"Shari, it's one of the very best things you can be."

Lies.
All of it—lies.

Tuesday

.

SEPTEMBER 5

12:12 A.M.

Rancho Bernardo, the adult community where my mother lived with her gentleman friend, Melvin Hunt, slept under a pale moon. When I was a child this land to the north of the city had been nothing but rolling hills inhabited by jackrabbits and coyotes; even after the spacious homes had spread across them, the nights here were eerily dark and quiet. But now the glow from the urban sprawl and the hum of the freeways told of population out of control. Fear had invaded the consciousness of the residents, too; I drove Pa's Suburban down deserted streets, past houses where placards bearing the logos of security firms were displayed.

Ma and Melvin's house was on a cul-de-sac. I parked haphazardly at the curb, ran up the flagstone walk, punched the bell. In minutes the outside light flashed on and Melvin peered through the door's small window. He registered surprise and let me in.

"Sharon! What're you doing here? It's after midnight." As he spoke he tightened the belt of his plaid robe; his thick gray hair, usually groomed to perfection, stuck up in un-

ruly peaks. His face was gaunt and he seemed much older
than when I'd visited last spring.

I said, "I need to talk with Ma."

"What's wrong? Has somebody else—"

"No, nothing like that. Please, will you tell her—"

"Tell me what?" My mother stepped into the tiled en-
tryway, clutching her pink velour robe at the neck. Her short
blond hair was as crisply styled as if she were going to a
dinner party, rather than rising to greet a midnight caller,
and her face had a youthful tightness. Irrelevantly I wondered if she had discovered some method of siphoning off
Melvin's vitality.

"Ma, we need to talk."

She came over and put a hand on my arm, peering anxiously at me. "Oh, you're a lot more upset than you sounded
on the phone!"

I looked down at her hand. Nothing youthful about it,
and the contrast with her face told me another secret Ma
had kept from me: she'd had cosmetic surgery.

"Yes, I'm upset," I said. "We need to sit down and talk."
I looked pointedly at the living room.

Ma nodded and asked Melvin, "Would you mind putting
some coffee on, dear?"

I said, "I don't want any coffee."

"Well, I need some. Come with me." She let go of my
arm, went into the room, turned on lights.

She'd redecorated since last spring, in rose and lilac and
cream, everything coordinated and in its place. Nothing at
all like the mismatched but comfortable clutter of the house
where I grew up. As I sat on the sofa and watched her curl
up in the chair across from me, I realized this was not the
mother I remembered. The woman who had loved to con-
coct huge meals in her kitchen and to dig barehanded in

her vegetable garden had vanished; in her place was a somewhat brittle lady whom you'd expect to find lunching or playing a leisurely round of golf at the country club. She'd even streamlined her nickname, Katie, to the more sophisticated Kay. A deliberate and complete transformation for her new life, and now I wondered what had been so bad about the old one.

"Sharon," she said, "what's got you in this state?"

I set my bag on the coffee table and took out the copy of the petition for adoption. "This."

As I held it up, she squinted and frowned. Then she recognized it and paled. "Where did you get that?" she whispered.

"It was in a box of legal papers in the garage. Pa told John that when he died he wanted me to go through the stuff."

An angry flush spread up Ma's neck. "Oh, damn you, Andy! Look what you've done!"

"He's dead, Ma. You don't have to get mad at him anymore."

"Don't you see? He set it up so you'd find that. For years he wanted you to know, but he didn't have the courage to tell you. So, as usual, he took the easy way out."

"Well, what about you? Weren't you taking the easy way out by *not* telling me?" God, I hated the pathetic little-girl whine in my voice!

She shook her head, put her fingertips to her lips.

"Did you think you were protecting me? From what?"

"Sharon, please, let it be. Destroy that document and forget you ever saw it."

"I can't destroy it! I can't forget. Who am I, Ma? Who was Baby Girl Smith?"

"I can't tell you that."

"Can't, or won't?"

". . . Both."

The hurt and anger I'd been holding in check broke loose. "Dammit, Ma, I need to know!"

"I'm sorry, Sharon. There are things . . . you don't understand."

"The only thing I *do* understand is that all those years, you and Pa lied to me: the story about me looking like Great-grandma; the nonsense about genetics. By your silence you lied to me every single day of my life! And you did it to protect yourselves."

"It isn't lying to—"

"Yes, it is. The one thing you managed to drum into my head with your good Catholic upbringing is that lying is wrong. Hell, according to the Church, it's a sin. What did you do when you went to confession? Admit to the priest that you'd lied to your daughter over and over and over?"

"Please, stop this!"

"Did John and Joey know and lie to me too? And the relatives—were they in on the conspiracy? Just how many other people knew and covered up for you?"

"Stop it!" She bowed her head, put her hands over her ears.

I raised my voice. "You can't block out what you don't want to hear. Not when it's the truth. And now that I've found out, I need to know who my parents were, why they gave me up, why you and Pa adopted me."

Melvin appeared in the archway, alarmed. I shook my head at him, motioned him off. He stayed where he was, eyes on my mother.

She looked up, her face twisted in pain, and in spite of my rage I felt a rush of love and pity for her. But then her lips grew taut and I saw a familiar steely resolve creep into her eyes.

"No, you do *not* need to know," she said. "Baby Girl Smith ceased to exist four days after she was born. You *are* Sharon McCone. I *am* your mother. Andy *was* your father. We sheltered you, fed you, clothed you—and loved you. That should be enough."

"But it's not enough, not now! Ma, I love you; don't push me away. Don't hide the truth from me. And for God's sake, don't tell me any more lies."

"I love you too. In many ways, your father and I loved you more than our own children."

Our own children.

I felt as if she'd slapped me.

Ma realized how her words had sounded and flashed a horrified glance at Melvin, who still hovered in the archway. "Sharon, I didn't mean—"

"Yes, you did. You meant it." I stood up.

"Don't go!" She started to get to her feet, but by then I was brushing past Melvin on my way to the door. As I opened it, I looked back at her; she made an imploring gesture with her hands, and when I didn't respond, her gaze faltered and fell.

It wasn't till I was speeding down the freeway that I identified what I'd seen in Ma's eyes during those final seconds.

She was afraid.

2:47 A.M.

"I didn't know!" John said.

"You must have! Where did you think Ma got me? She wasn't pregnant."

"Shar, I was eight years old—"

"And you sure as hell knew where babies came from. Ma's good Catholic friends got pregnant on a yearly basis."

We were standing toe to toe in the living room of his house in Lemon Grove, where I'd gone after driving all around San Diego in a near-blind fury. When I stormed in without knocking, he was hanging up the phone. Ma, he said. She'd called three times since I left Rancho Bernardo, giving him a bit more of the story in each conversation and finally begging him to find me and calm me down.

Instead, he was only making me angrier. "Go ahead, why don't you—lie some more! But *this* doesn't lie." I shook the petition for adoption under his nose.

"Stop it!" He snatched the document from my hand and grabbed me by the shoulders, crumpling it. "You're pissed at Ma, but she's not here, so you're taking it out on me. Just *stop* it."

I tried to pull away, but he held on fast, hurting me. His eyes were wild with frustration—fear, too. This was my brother, I loved him, except that he wasn't really my brother, and my finding that document had turned us into strangers. Adversaries, maybe.

My own fear welled up and spilled out in a rush of tears. John pulled me close and let me cry, stroking my hair, and after a bit I realized he was crying too. Some of my anger dissipated. I stepped back and regarded him while fumbling for a tissue. "Now, aren't we a sorry sight," I said.

"The worst. I don't know about you, but I could use a drink."

I nodded absently. The room had begun to seem close and hot, and my equilibrium was off. I ran the back of my hand over my forehead, felt dampness. "I can't stay in here."

"We'll talk outside. I'll be right with you." When I didn't move, John made a shooing motion. "Go!"

I went, stood at the foot of the steps, looking around. On the side of the knoll where John's small yellow house sat was a bench, old and splintery, that he and Joey had stolen years before from a downtown bus stop. When I lowered myself onto it, my limbs felt leaden and I had a premonition of what it would feel like to be a very old woman.

The night was clear and cold. Below me spread the pinkish streetlights of the quiet neighborhood and San Diego's nearby Encanto district. They backlit the yucca trees that crowded the downslope, their clumps of long leaves leaning together like the heads of shaggy-haired people in hushed conversation. A couple of yards over, a cat screeched and another replied in kind.

John came out with two glasses, thrust one into my hand, and sat, placing a piece of paper on the seat between us. The petition for adoption, smoothed out as best he could. I didn't pick it up; instead I raised my glass and sniffed. Bourbon, what I used to drink before I decided to cut back on the hard stuff. The first sip burned my throat, the second went down just fine. Maybe I'd get drunk and blot out all of this.

"Okay," I said after a minute, "you didn't know. But you must've suspected something."

"Well, early on I wondered why you didn't look like Joey or me. And when Charlene was born, I started asking questions. Ma and Pa gave me that stuff about you inheriting more of Great-grandma's genes than us, and later we had a unit on genetics in science class that more or less confirmed it was possible."

"And that's it? You never wondered again?"

"Sure I did. Especially when the rest of us started having kids. I mean, Karen and I had our three, Charlene her six, Patsy her three. No recessive gene ever came out in any of them. Besides, you're different in other ways."

"Such as?"

". . . You're hardworking. Focused. Ambitious. You got great grades in high school, put yourself through college, bought a house, started your own business. You've really made something of your life."

"And you haven't? Mr. Paint is one of the most successful contracting companies in the county. Charlene's going to get her M.B.A. next year, and Patsy's a partner in two restaurants now."

"Yeah, but then there's Joey. Sometimes I think it's a wonder he can feed himself. And the rest of us came by our work ethic late in life. Yours was always there. You never fucked up like Joey and I did."

"Well, in those days it wasn't customary for girls to steal stuff or get into brawls in bars."

"No, but you also didn't screw every guy who came along, like Charlene. Or run away from home and do drugs, like Patsy."

"Maybe I just didn't carry that kind of behavior to the extremes they did."

"Hey, I'm your big brother; I don't want to hear about what you did."

I looked solemnly at him. *Was* he still my big brother, or had the discovery of that document nullified the relationship?

After a moment I said, "Didn't you think that if I was adopted I had a right to know?"

"I thought about that a few times, yes. But what was I supposed to do? I had no proof, and you didn't suspect anything. Besides, I wanted to believe the genetic explanation."

"Why?"

"Because I love you, dummy. I wanted you to be my natural sister."

". . . I love you too." I put a tentative hand on his arm, squeezed it. "Okay—d'you think the relatives knew?"

"If they did, nobody ever said anything about it in my hearing—and you know how hard it was for that crowd to keep their mouths shut."

"They must've known, though. The family was always around: Aunt Clarisse and Uncle Ed, Great-aunt Fenella, Grandpa, Uncle Jim and Aunt Susan. Even Great-grandma, for a few years. They'd've known Ma wasn't pregnant."

In the darkness I felt, rather than saw, John shrug.

"What d'you remember about the nine months before I was born? Was Pa stateside or overseas?" In the Navy, he'd spent much of his time on long deployments in the Pacific.

"I don't— Well, of course, that might explain it. For most of the time Ma should've been pregnant with you, Pa was in the Philippines. And Ma's mother was sick—she died early the next year—so she spent a lot of time with her up in San Luis Obispo. Joey and I lived with Ed and Clarisse— no picnic." Our Aunt Clarisse—Ma's brother's wife—had hated children and taken it out on all of us in small, sadistic ways.

"Joey and I hardly ever saw Ma," John added, "and neither did the relatives. When Pa came home a couple of weeks before you were born, he said Ma was having a difficult pregnancy and asked Ed and Clarisse to keep us till the two of you were home from the hospital."

So the whole thing had been carefully and deliberately orchestrated. A well-manufactured lie. But even lies of the finest workmanship have a flaw, if you look hard enough for it.

"John, are Aunt Susan and Uncle Jim still living in Jackson?"

"Yeah. He still owns the bowling alley—no, we're supposed to call them bowling *centers* now. Why?"

"Just curious."

"Right. Shar, what're you gonna do?"

I didn't reply.

"Goddamn it, you're gonna investigate this."

"That's what I do."

"Yes, but for clients. People who pay. You shouldn't be—"

"Why not? It's not as if I'm a doctor attempting to perform brain surgery on myself."

"But what if . . . ?"

"Yes?"

"Well, what if you find out something unpleasant? Or just plain nasty? There has to be a reason Ma and Pa kept your adoption secret."

"If I do, I'll deal with it."

"Are you sure?"

"The only thing I'm sure of is that there's nothing worse than not knowing who you are or where you came from."

"You *know* who you are."

"Apparently I don't know as much as I thought I did."

We sat in silence for a long time, and after a while the stars paled and the yucca trees began to take on greater definition. John spoke first.

"Promise me one thing."

"What?"

"Promise—cross your heart, and if you lie, I swear I'll get horrible old Aunt Clarisse to come back and haunt you— promise that no matter what you find out, you'll always be my sister."

I looked into his eyes, saw love overshadowed by anxiety. He was my brother, no question about it.

"I promise." And I crossed my heart, just as I had so many times when we were children.

1:30 P.M.

"McCone, I've been trying to get hold of you. Don't you ever turn on your cellular?"

"Couldn't. I just got off my flight from San Diego. I'm at Oakland. Listen, Ripinsky, are you planning to use the plane in the next couple of days?"

"Don't think so. Why?"

"I need to take it, at least overnight."

"Wait a minute. When're you coming back to the office?"

"How are things there?"

"Busy. I've got the feeling I'm barely holding the agency together. Christ, Ted's doing a better job than I am."

"So let him."

"This isn't like you—"

"Look, if you don't want me to take the plane, just say so!"

Silence.

I said, "It was my understanding that it was *our* plane, not just—"

"Okay, what's the matter?"

"I don't know what you mean."

"Yes, you do. You're all wound up, and it isn't about the agency or the plane—or your father dying."

I couldn't even fool him on the phone. "All right, it's not, but I can't talk about it right now. I've got something I need to do first."

"Then go do it. But call me."

"I will, tonight. I'll explain everything then."

I switched off the phone and pressed my forehead against the cool metal door of the stall in the women's room, where I'd hidden to make the call. Maybe I was old-fashioned, but I'd never adapted to the common—and annoying—practice of talking on the thing while striding through airports or sitting in restaurants or pushing my grocery cart.

Hy was right: I was all wound up. But he couldn't suspect what I'd found out, or that one of the things that had me in this state was the prospect of telling him about my discovery. As unlikely as it seemed, on some level I was afraid that the news I was adopted would make him look at me differently, perhaps wonder who this woman he loved really was. And why not? It was making *me* look at myself differently, making *me* wonder.

After a moment I pulled myself together and went to fetch my car to drive to the general aviation terminal at North Field, where our new Cessna 170B—a sexy red one with blue accent trim—waited in the tie-downs.

When Hy's old Citabria had been totaled last winter, we decided we wanted a bigger, faster, more practical aircraft. But after test-flying dozens of planes and finding serious fault with each, we realized how much we missed the old high-winged tail-dragger. Then Sara Grimly, a flight instructor at Los Alegres Municipal Airport, where I'd learned to fly, heard of our dilemma and called me. Friends of hers had a special plane up for sale, and she thought we ought to take a look at it.

Two-five-two-seven-Tango was also a tail-dragger, and a beauty. The couple who owned it had rescued the nearly fifty-year-old aircraft from languishing in a derelict yet structurally sound state at a small airfield in North Carolina and flown it at risk of life and limb to Los Alegres, where they then embarked on the most ambitious restoration project of their lives. The engine was replaced, upgrading it to 180 horsepower; the dashboard was redesigned and loaded with the latest instrumentation; ailing and ancient radios were traded for state-of-the-art communications gear; a portion of the tail section was rebuilt. Then came the cosmetics: new seats, paint, upholstery, and carpets. By the time Hy and I test-flew the plane, what the owners described as once having been a "disreputable tin can" had been transformed into a magnificent machine, capable of flying 120 miles per hour—rather than being outdistanced by cars on the roads below—and of holding three adults with luggage or four without.

Plus it handled like a dream. I soared effortlessly above the hills through the airspace where I'd once been a struggling student pilot, glided feather-light onto the runway where I'd often committed what my instructor had called "arrivals"—as distinguished from real landings. And I lusted after Two-five-two-seven-Tango. One glance at Hy told me he was similarly enthralled.

So, we asked the owners after we taxied up to their hangar, why were they selling this paragon of a plane, the fruit of three years' expense and labor?

The couple exchanged glances. Hy and I did too: something wrong here?

Then the man confessed: Last month they'd traveled to Louisiana and again risked life and limb ferrying a derelict Cessna Bird Dog—originally manufactured for the Army in 1950 as a reconnaissance and observation aircraft—to Los Alegres. It was now tucked in the hangar awaiting rehabilitation once the 170B sold.

Yes, the woman admitted, some people never learn.

We made a deal and shook on it before Two-seven-Tango's engine cooled.

Now, as every time I arrived at the field and saw the Cessna tied there, I felt a fierce stir of pride—doting mama admiring her offspring. Leave it to me to have an airplane, rather than a child.

It was better I hadn't procreated, though. Lord knew what kind of genes I might have passed on.

I stowed my things in the backseat, preflighted, and soon was airborne, complying with the controller's instructions to turn right and follow the Nimitz Freeway over the city. Once the ATC terminated communication, I set a north-easterly course for Amador County Airport. The meandering channels and sculpted islands of the Sacramento Delta lay below me, and then the vast, flat valley crisscrossed by farm roads. I noted landmarks to stay on course, but otherwise ignored the scenery, preoccupied with my thoughts and feelings.

Usually when in the air I experienced a tremendous sense of freedom and control; no one could lay claim to me there, no earthbound problem was so serious that altitude didn't make me capable of coping. But today I felt trapped by insurmountable circumstances. I flew joylessly and tentatively, chafing at a strong headwind that slowed my airspeed.

Stupid to let a piece of paper dislocate my life. Stupid to let other people's falsehoods make *me* feel false.

Just plain stupid.

4:10 P.M.

Jackson was nestled in the foothills of the Sierra Nevada, the old Motherlode gold country. A former mining town with a historic business district and the beginnings of small-city sprawl, it was flanked on the west by wheat-colored ranchland dotted with oak and madrone, and on the east by forested hills. As I drove my rental car south on Route 49, signs along the highway warned that fire danger was high today.

My Uncle Jim hadn't been at the bowling center on the southeast edge of town—taking the day off, the woman at the desk told me. So I kept going into the wooded countryside to the small ranch he and Aunt Susan had bought after he quit the pro circuit and built Jim McCone's Lanes. It was three miles or so off the highway, bordered by split-rail fences, with a long graveled drive leading past grazing cattle to the redwood-and-fieldstone house. Hummingbird feeders hanging from the eaves by the door glinted in the afternoon sun. For a moment I remained in the car, watching the play of light.

Jim and Susan had always been my favorite relatives: easy-going with fine senses of humor, understanding of the difficulties we kids had growing up, even though they had no children of their own. But as I flew up here I'd begun to wonder if there hadn't been a touch of condescension—maybe even pity—in their treatment of me. After all, I wasn't really a relation, had probably come from bad stock. And then I'd begun to fear that my confrontation with them would turn as unpleasant as the one with Ma. And finally I'd begun to think I'd developed a full-blown case of paranoia.

Finally I took a deep breath, got out of the car, went up and rang the bell.

After a bit the door opened and Jim's ruddy face appeared, looking so like my father's in his younger days that I felt a sharp wrenching in my gut. He peered at me with some anxiety, seemed relieved at what he saw, and said, "We've been expecting you."

"Oh? Why—"

"Katie—pardon me, Kay—called. Come in, please. Suzy and I were just cracking a beer on the deck. Spent the day getting our spring bulbs in, and that's enough work for a couple of geezers like us."

I remained where I was, stunned by what my mother had done. The word was out, the willful silence imposed. Now I'd never get any information from Jim and Susan.

"Come on now," he said, holding the door wide. "Whatever's happening, we're on your side."

I followed him into the cool house and through a series of rooms to a deck that overlooked forestland and distant mountain peaks. Susan sat on a lounge chair in shorts and bare feet, her gray hair tousled. She gave me a look as penetrating as Jim's earlier one, glanced at him, and nodded in silent agreement. "We were wondering when you'd turn up," she said.

"Ma must've guessed I'd want to talk with you. John knew I was coming, but he'd've never told her. What'd she say?"

"That you were all bent out of shape over something you found out after Andy died, and behaving irrationally."

"Great." I sat down on the chair next to her.

"Of course we discounted that. We've never known you to be irrational."

"As usual, Ma's exaggerating."

"Well, you know your mother."

No, I don't. Not the way I thought I did.

Jim had gone back into the house; now he returned with a glass of white wine for me—remembering what I drank in spite of not having seen me for several years. No condescension or pity here, but thumbs-up on my paranoia.

I asked, "Did Ma tell you what I found out?"

Jim reclaimed his chair, shook his head. "Nope. And after seeing you, I'd say Katie's the crazy one. What's all this about?"

I took the petition for adoption from my bag and handed it to him. He fished his glasses from his shirt pocket, read it, and whistled softly. His surprise seemed genuine. "Suzy, take a look at this."

She scanned it, frowning. "Incredible!"

"That's what I thought when I first found it," I said, "but then things began to make sense. I confronted Ma, but she refused to explain." Briefly I described Ma's reaction and repeated what John had told me about the time when she allegedly was pregnant with me.

"Well, they kept us in the dark too," Jim said. "This is sure a shock."

"Why do you think they did that? It would've been so much easier if everybody—including me—had known the truth."

He looked at Susan, shrugged.

"Did Ma say anything else when she called?" I asked.

"Told me you'd probably ask a lot of questions that we wouldn't be able to answer. Said we shouldn't take everything you said at face value, it was a complicated situation. She thought you'd want to talk about the past, and would we please not mention Fenella."

"Great-aunt Fenella?" She'd kept house for my grandfather and helped care for Pa and Jim when their mother died of cancer when Jim was a baby. "What on earth does she have to do with this?"

"Damned if I know."

"Could she have been—?"

"Your birth mother?" Jim glanced at Susan.

"Hardly," she said. "By the time you were born Fenella was close to fifty. And even if she were still physically capable of conceiving, she'd proven by her track record that she knew how to prevent *that*."

I pictured Fenella, who had died in a mountain-climbing accident at the age of sixty-four. Although she never married, she'd had more than her fair share of lovers and didn't fit the profile of the maiden aunt in any respect. "Then what *does* she have to do with it?"

Jim said, "Interesting question."

"Are you willing to talk about her, in spite of Ma asking you not to?"

They looked at each other, and then Jim's eyes started to gleam. "I've always been fond of Katie," he said, "but ever since she hooked up with the King of the Laundromats, she's turned into an imperious pain in the ass. We'd be delighted to discuss Fenella."

I was exhausted from my sleepless night before, so shortly after dinner I excused myself and went to Jim and Susan's cozy guest room, where I curled up in bed and thought over the things they'd told me.

While none of Ma and Pa's friends and relatives had seen her after what was supposedly the fourth month of her pregnancy, Great-aunt Fenella visited her several times at her mother's home in San Luis Obispo. Fenella herself had spent much of that time nursing her own mother, my Shoshone great-grandmother, Mary McCone, through a bout with pneumonia. The two were close, closer than most mothers and daughters.

Fenella, Jim claimed, was like me in many ways: adventurous, outspoken, unconventional, and inquisitive. When Pa and Jim were young, she'd bundle them into her car and take them camping or fishing on the spur of the moment. After they grew up, she traveled the world by freighter. In spite of many offers, she refused to marry, although for a time she "lived in sin" with an actor. She drank hard, drove fast, and took up mountain climbing in her forties. At fifty she enrolled at San Diego State, and four years later received her degree in anthropology—an area of interest that stemmed from her fascination with her Shoshone roots. At one point in the 1950s she visited the reservation where her mother's relatives lived.

That piece of information surprised me. My parents had claimed Mary McCone never spoke of the years before she appeared in Flagstaff, Arizona, and joined my great-grandfather on his trek west. She'd disavowed her heritage, became a good Catholic matron, and never once looked back. But now it seemed she must have discussed that past with her daughter.

What reservation? I asked Jim. He didn't know. What had Fenella done there? Who had she met? She never said; she had a secretive streak.

And that was it. Not much to go on. Susan's and Jim's memories might be inaccurate, colored or faded by time. But at least I now had a clearer picture of a woman I could have liked, had I taken the time to know her. I'd only been thirteen when she died, a self-absorbed and conformist age; then she was simply the relative in the too-short skirt and too-big hair who'd once embarrassed me when my girlfriends and I encountered her at the mall.

It was getting late, and I realized I hadn't called Hy as promised—an oversight no doubt prompted by my discomfort with telling him I was adopted. Now I braced myself, dialed, and reached him at my house. My reluctance to talk with him vanished as I related my story. If anything, he seemed less surprised by it than the others I'd told.

"Well, families keep worse secrets," he said. "How're you gonna deal with this?"

"God, I don't know. Keep asking questions, I guess."

"Why not go up against your mother again?"

"No! Not after what she did today, calling Jim and Susan. To tell the truth, I'm not sure I ever want to lay eyes on her again."

"That's just anger talking."

"Don't I have a right to be angry?"

"You have a right to whatever you're feeling. But I don't think you should cut her off till you know the whole story."

". . . You're being wise, as usual."

He ignored the comment. "What about the lawyer who handled your adoption? Maybe he could tell you something."

"I checked before I left San Diego. He's long dead, but I doubt he would have, anyway."

"Old family friends?"

"I made phone calls to a few. None of them seemed to know anything. If Ma and Pa hid my adoption from relatives, they'd certainly have hidden it from friends."

"I've heard there're bulletin boards on the Internet, where adoptees can post, in case their biological parents are looking for them."

"Maybe I'll try that. But it's such a long shot. Jesus, Ripinsky, I'm an *investigator* and I don't know what to do!"

Silence. Then: "McCone, could be you're going about this wrong."

"How so?"

"Well, from what you say, you've been listening to what

people're willing to tell you, and it's not much. Maybe you should listen to what they're *not* willing to tell."

"How d'you mean?"

"You've known these people all your life. You're tuned in to their personalities, their ways of thinking, subtle nuances. Tune out their words and listen to what's hidden in the spaces between them. To the pauses, the hesitations. Picture them at the times when they won't look you in the eye."

"Interesting approach."

"You try it. Listen to the silence. It can tell you everything."

I slept fitfully, plagued by disturbing dreams, one of which brought me fully awake before midnight. It was a vivid image of a circle: golden, perfect, its arc moving from me to Great-aunt Fenella, then to Mary McCone, and back to me. A circle connecting the three of us and excluding all others.

LISTENING . . .

"*Who was Baby Girl Smith?*"

"*I can't tell you that.*"

"*Can't, or won't?*"

". . . *Both.*"

"*Dammit, Ma, I need to know!*"

"I'm sorry, Sharon. There are things . . . you don't under-stand."

Those are the silences: the hesitations before Ma said the words "both" and "you don't understand." Listen to them, picture her.

She's drawing back into her chair, away from my questions. There's a tremor around her mouth, and her eyes are half closed. What's the emotion she's trying to hide? Why has she laced her fingers together?

What is it she's *not* saying?

"I can't tell you because there are things Andy and I weren't told. And I won't tell you because I'm afraid of what those things might be. Andy shared your obsession with the truth; he hated that we didn't know everything. That's why he left the document where you'd be sure to find it—so you'd un-cover that truth."

Yes, maybe.

"And that's it? You never wondered again?"

"Sure I did. Especially when the rest of us started having kids. I mean, Karen and I had our three, Charlene her six, Patsy her three. No recessive gene ever came out in any of them. Besides, you're different in other ways."

"Such as?"

". . . You're hardworking. Focused. Ambitious. . . ."

Another silence, before John starts reciting all the ways I'm different. Something he doesn't want to say, for fear of hurting me or provoking a scene like before?

Could be. That kind of scene was nothing new. He and I fought a lot when we were growing up.

"You're a spoiled brat, Shar!"

"Am not!"

"Yeah, you are. You get away with stuff none of the rest of us can."

"Do not!"

"Yes, you do. You're Pa's favorite. He doesn't give any of us special nicknames, but with you it's always 'Shari this' and 'Shari that' and 'My little girl gets such good grades.' "

"So? You want I should've got kicked out of Catholic school like Joey and you?"

"Spoiled brat! Why're you the favorite?"

Is it the memory of old favoritism that lives in John's silence? Could be. I always received special treatment.

And then there's that folder in Pa's box of legal documents: all my report cards and copies of my diplomas.

I can understand the special treatment: guilt, because of all the lies. But why'd you save those things, Pa? Why did they mean more to you than those of your natural children?

Or were you saving them for someone? My birth parents, in case they ever found me?

"What reservation did Fenella visit, Jim?"

"I don't know."

"What did she do there? Who did she meet?"

". . . She never said. She had a secretive streak, you know."

There's that silence again. And the look that passes between Jim and Susan. They've always exchanged those swift, telling glances, communicated on a nonverbal level. Jim wants to leave a party, he looks at Susan, she eases them out the door. Susan wants to change the tack of a conversation, she looks at Jim, Jim launches into one of his bowling anecdotes. So what does this particular glance mean?

He's remembered something, and when he looks at Susan, she remembers it too. It's not good, and suddenly they think they may have talked too much. They're feeling protective toward me, so Jim steers the conversation to Fenella's idiosyncrasies, hoping I'll forget her reservation visit.

Not too likely. Not too damn likely I'll forget or ignore any of those silences.

Thursday

·

SEPTEMBER 7

1:32 P.M.

"Here's the stuff you asked for on the Shoshones."

Mick set the file on my desk with a thump. It was a big one, about two inches thick. The stack of manila folders on my side table was high, and growing: articles on genealogy; lists of databases; printouts from Web sites; text of Division 13 of the California Family Code, regulating adoptions. That last one had been slow going; I often amused myself by dipping into law books, but after spending an hour with the civil statutes, I had to admit that I found the criminal code more diverting.

"All this," I said to Mick, "on one little tribe?" I'd asked for the information because of my growing conviction that Fenella's visit to the reservation was directly connected with my adoption, but I hadn't expected to be inundated.

He propped his hip on the edge of the desk, looking smug, as he always did when he knew more about a subject than I. "They're not a little tribe, Shar. There're all sorts of Shoshones: Bannocks, Lemhis, Northern, Eastern, Duckwater, Elys, Fallon Paiutes. And they're scattered all over

Wyoming, Idaho, Montana, the Pacific Northwest, Nevada, Arizona, here in California. I got you everything I could off the Net, plus ordered some books."

"On what?" I rubbed my forehead over my right eyebrow, where a headache was rapidly blossoming.

"History, customs, religion, arts and crafts. The reservation system and its current status. I figure if you're gonna trace our family's roots, you ought to know as much as possible."

Mick thought I'd assigned him this project out of a simple interest in the family background brought on by Pa's death. He was still reeling from that loss, and I hadn't wanted to further shake him up by revealing I was adopted. Not yet, anyway.

"Don't look so discouraged," he added. "It's pretty easy reading. Most of the stuff off the Net is kinda sketchy."

I eyed the folder disbelievingly. In college I'd been a fanatical researcher, often emerging crosseyed from the library at closing time to realize I'd stood up a date. But nowadays the volume of information available by computer was formidable. By the time I'd plowed through it and determined where and how to start my search, my biological parents would be long dead (if they weren't already), I'd be an old lady, and my agency would have gone to hell because of my inattention.

As if to prove the point, the phone buzzed and Ted's voice said, "Glenn Solomon on line two."

"Tell him I'll call back."

"He says it's urgent."

I sighed. With Glenn, a prominent criminal defense attorney who regularly channeled business my way, it was always urgent. "Okay, I'll talk with him. Thanks." As I picked up, Mick saluted me and went out onto the iron catwalk that fronted our second-story suite, his somewhat melancholy whistle echoing off the vaulted ceiling of the pier.

Half an hour later I'd taken down the details of the embezzlement case Glenn was defending, explained them to Charlotte Keim, my best investigator in the financial area, and told her to set up an appointment with Glenn's client. Then I dialed John's office number in San Diego.

"Hey, it's my afternoon for sisters," he said. "I just talked with Charlene and Patsy."

"When did Charlene and Vic get back from London?"

"Yesterday. They cut the trip short; she's taking Pa's death really hard."

"And Patsy?"

"Well, you know how she keeps things bottled up inside. Neither of them has heard from Joey. I'm starting to think we'll never get to tell him about Pa."

"He'll show up when he's ready." Last winter he'd left his job as a waiter in McMinnville, Oregon, and hadn't surfaced till June, when he sent Ma a birthday card from Eureka, a lumber town in northern California.

"Yeah, I guess so." John hesitated. "Ma's called me a couple of times."

"Oh? What did she want?"

"For me to talk some sense into you."

"And do you plan to try?"

"I couldn't if I wanted to."

"Did you tell Charlene and Patsy what I found out?"

"Not my place to, but I'm sure Ma'll spread the word of what an ungrateful child you are."

"She *said* that?"

"Implied."

"Jesus!"

--

"So what'd you find out from Jim and Susan?"

I told him, adding, "I'd like to ask a favor of you. Go over to Pa's house and look through those legal papers. See if there's anything like a marriage license for Great-grandma and -grandpa. Or birth certificates for Fenella and Grandpa James. Something that'll show what Mary McCone's birth name was. And while you're at it, see if Pa kept anything of Fenella's."

A long pause. "Shar, maybe Ma's right. Can't you just let go of this? Aren't the rest of us family enough for you?"

"It's not family I'm after."

"What then?"

A question I'd been asking myself. Identity, I supposed. A history. The truth. And something more that I couldn't yet put a name to.

"Just take a look, will you? Please?"

"Only if you say 'Pretty please with peanut butter on it.'"

Was he deliberately trying to remind me of our shared childhood, hoping to reinforce the bond between us?

"Say it!"

I sighed. "Pretty please with peanut butter on it. The super-chunk kind."

9:47 P.M.

From where she crouched on the back of the sofa, Alice the calico cat regarded me with slitted eyes. On the hearth rug her orange tabby brother, Ralph, telegraphed unease with the tip of his tail. Both had picked up on my restless tension and were probably afraid they'd done something to provoke it.

I dropped the file Mick had put together on the Shoshones on the floor. Alice levitated and streaked for the kitchen. Ralph tried to play it cool by yawning and stretching before he followed. When in doubt, check the food bowl for crunchies.

Hy was staying at his ranch in the high desert country tonight, so I'd taken advantage of his absence to plow through the mound of information I'd amassed, starting with adoption and ending with Native Americans. The adoption and genealogy material was dry and boring, often incomprehensible, but the Shoshones were another story: Photographs accompanying the text Mick had provided convinced me they were my people. Made me suspect that at least one of my birth parents was somebody Fenella had met on that trip to the reservation.

There wasn't a whole lot of consensus about the tribe, and that pleased me because it indicated complexity. The name was variously spelled *Shoshone* and *Shoshoni*, and some writers called them Snake Indians. Historians—mostly non-Indian—lauded them for their friendship toward the white man, while citing epithets applied by their more warlike brethren that ranged from "false Indians" to "dirty dog eaters." It didn't help their stock with other tribes that one of their women, Sacajawea, volunteered to guide the Lewis and Clark expedition to the Pacific coast.

One fact about the Shoshones put me off: their neighbors, the Comanches, introduced them to the horse in the early eighteenth century, and they took to the animal with enthusiasm, expanding their hunting and fishing territory west from Wyoming's Bighorn Mountains to Idaho's Snake River, and south from the Yellowstone River to the Uinta Mountains of Utah. I, on the other hand, flat-out hated horses. The critters sensed right off that they could push me around, and in my limited experience with them I'd been stepped on, knocked over, thrown, and kidnapped by a recalcitrant beast that galloped miles down the beach near Half Moon Bay, then refused to return to the stables.

The Shoshone religion was based on the belief in one Creator, visions, and dreams, and every year was expressed in the Sun Dance ceremony.

Well, as far as I was concerned, the jury was still out on the Creator, but I did rely on my dreams for insights into my cases.

This religion was said to foster courage, self-reliance, and wisdom. The Shoshones were skilled in dealing with life's problems in a difficult and often hostile environment.

Wise I wasn't, but any good investigator has to be brave and self-reliant. And as for dealing with a difficult and hostile environment, as an urbanite I contended on a daily basis. Thrived on it, actually.

During the reservation era, the Shoshone were forced onto three reserves: Wind River in west central Wyoming; Fort Hall on the Snake River in southeastern Idaho; and Lemhi Valley in northern Idaho. In 1907 the latter was closed and the few remaining Lemhi removed to Fort Hall, thus ending a decades-old struggle to stay on their ancestral lands.

That meant the reservation Fenella had visited was either Wind River or Fort Hall. I went to the bookcase, took down my atlas, and located them. To my Californian's eye they seemed remote, isolated, and I thought of all the time I'd need and distance I'd have to cover in order to find my roots.

It was after ten now, and John hadn't called me back. He'd said he would go over to Pa's house right after work, but I supposed something more pressing had come up. Either that, or he hadn't found anything and didn't feel any urgency about letting me know. If the latter was the case, what would be my next logical step . . . ?

The phone rang. I looked at the base unit, saw the receiver wasn't there. Just as the call was about to go to the machine, I located it on the kitchen table under a bundle of clothes I'd put out to take to the dry cleaner.

John. "Sorry I took so long to get back to you. A client came into the office just as I was closing up, insisted on taking me to dinner. Anyway, I'm at Pa's. There's a box of stuff here that looks like it belonged to Fenella. What should I do with it?"

"Can you FedEx it first thing in the morning?"

"Sure. There's also a marriage certificate for Great-grandma and -grandpa, tucked inside a family Bible that nobody's written in since Uncle Jim was born. Her maiden name was Tendoy."

Tendoy. Somewhere in my reading I'd run across it.

Tendoy was chief of the Lemhi Shoshones from 1863 until his death in 1907, a buffalo hunter with close ties to the white community and a fondness for the white man's whiskey. He spearheaded the Lemhis' efforts to stay on their land in the Idaho River valley. Through periods of extreme privation, when allotments of food and clothing from Washington were inexplicably given to less friendly tribes and withheld from the Lemhi, he kept his people together and eventually saw the establishment of a small reservation. But, as usual, the government stinted: the land allotted to the Lemhi amounted to one-tenth of an acre per individual, as opposed to one and a half acres at Fort Hall—not nearly enough for the agriculture-based existence the federal powers-that-be were determined to impose on the tribe.

When the governmental push for the Lemhi to move to Fort Hall began, Tendoy vowed he would never do so; and after many lobbying trips to officials throughout Idaho and Montana, as well as to the nation's capital, he kept that promise by falling off his horse into a creek and dying of exposure—drunk on whiskey supplied by an unscrupulous white man.

As he lay dying in the creek bed, Chief Tendoy may well have reflected that the humiliation of such a death was nothing compared to the humiliation of his tribe at the hands of the U.S. government.

I stood in the door of my home office, surveying the new iMac computer that looked out of place on my old-fashioned desk. The machine seemed to call to me, a siren song of cyber-language.

You and I are friends now! Let's take it further!

Dammit, why had I—in a fit of boredom—taught myself to use the Macintosh that Hy kept at our seaside retreat in Mendocino County? If I hadn't gone up alone one fateful week last summer to monitor our contractor's progress on the new house we were building there, I'd still be pure.

Think how good we'll be together!

And then why had I returned home and bought the iMac? Indulged in the guilty pleasure of selecting printer and software—to say nothing of color? (Tangerine.) Then taken the machine home, made it comfortable, honed my technique, learned the delicious curves of the Information Highway?

Disgusting, McCone. Just disgusting.

Come on over here and play with me!

Seduced. Shamefully seduced.

You can do anything you want with me! Anything at all!

I went over, pushed the power button. The machine gave a happy, welcoming chime, and soon the screen glowed.

Anything!

Not tonight. It's late.

Anything . . .

Including a trace on Mary Tendoy McCone's surviving relatives.

Let's do it now!

I reached for the mouse—rolling over for the very technology I'd sworn never to embrace.

White pages/yellow pages. Click on white.

City & state. Fort Hall, Idaho.

Party. Tendoy.

Searching.

Thirteen Tendoys in the Bingham County directory.

Print.

White pages/yellow pages. Click on white.

City & state. Fort Washakie, Wyoming.

Party. Tendoy.

Searching.

Two Tendoys listed in Fremont County.

Print.

Late now. Too late to start calling. But tomorrow . . .

Friday

•

SEPTEMBER 8

8:22 A.M.

"I don't know nothin' about no Tendoys. It's my old man's name, and he's long gone."

"Lady, do you know what time it is here? I work nights, and I just got to bed."

"Chief Tendoy? Never heard of him."

"It's a common surname. As I understand, the chief had many descendants, but most of us don't know too much about him."

"Sorry, we don't accept telemarketing calls."

"I'm so out of touch with my Indian side that I couldn't find it with both hands."

"I think Chief Tendoy had a daughter named Mary by one of his wives, but I couldn't swear to it."

"Why don't you try Dwight Tendoy, down in Nampa? Genealogy's his hobby."

"Yes," Dwight Tendoy said, "the chief had a daughter named Mary by his third wife, Ta Gwah Wee. The girl was kidnapped by a corrupt Indian agent, John Blaine, in 1888. You say she was your great-grandmother?"

"That's right. She met my great-grandfather in Flagstaff that same year and went with him to California."

"Interesting. No one ever found out what happened to her, but John Blaine was murdered near Fort Hall in 1891. The consensus was that two of Tendoy's sons had a hand in it."

"Mr. Tendoy, do you know where I might find someone who could tell me more about Mary?"

"Hmmm. There's Elwood Farmer. His mother was Tendoy's youngest daughter, married a white man. Elwood's living in Saint Ignatius, on the Flathead Reservation in Montana. He married a woman from there."

"D'you have a phone number for him?"

"No, but I have a feeling you'll do better if you just show up and talk with him in person."

"Why?"

"Well, Elwood's an unusual man."

"How so?"

"You'll see, Ms. McCone. You'll see."

Go today? Wait till tomorrow when the box of Fenella's stuff is supposed to arrive, see if there's a more promising lead in it?

But what's a lead from the dead past, compared to meeting a living, breathing relative of Mary Tendoy McCone?

Go today.

4:10 P.M.

Montana's big sky was overcast by darkly bruised cumuli as I turned north on Highway 93 outside Missoula. The two-lane road paralleled a railroad track and ran through a big bowl-like valley surrounded by low, folded hills. Lodgepole pine crowded in on dirt roads that led to small ranches with prefab houses or doublewide trailers. In the distance I could see the Rockies: stark and one-dimensional, like blue-black cardboard cutouts of mountains.

I was feeling mildly depressed—a late-afternoon sinking spell brought on by the weather—as well as nervous about approaching Elwood Farmer. Normally I had no difficulty striking a rapport with total strangers, but usually I did so for professional reasons, and this meeting would be deeply personal, perhaps emotional on my side. I wished that Dwight Tendoy had told me more about Farmer, but before I could press for further details, he'd had another call, given me Farmer's address, and ended our conversation.

Arlee, the first town on the Flathead Reservation, was tiny—little more than a scattering of small frame houses, a bar, and a red water tower. I passed through quickly. As I neared St. Ignatius my nervousness intensified, and I stared at my surroundings as if they were an alien landscape. Here in Indian country lived my people, and yet I had nothing in common with them. I'd been raised to think of myself as Scotch-Irish with a touch of Native American blood, and nothing in my background had prepared me to understand their world or way of thinking. Frankly, I felt so dislocated that I wanted to make a U-turn, head back to Missoula, and catch the first plane home to San Francisco.

A sign for St. Ignatius appeared and then, on the left side of the highway, a harbinger of tourism: Doug Allard's Flathead Indian Museum. The town itself was on the right, so I headed that way. Church, community center, shops, bars, cafés, medical and dental clinics, school. A classic movie theater had been turned into a realty office. Most of the buildings were old and false-fronted, with roofed porches; they could have been the set of a Western movie. I'd driven through reservations before, both in California and Arizona, and found this one very different; there was no sense of a closed community, and many of the people on the streets were white. From some hastily assembled information on the Flathead reserve that I'd read on the plane, I'd learned that outsiders had acquired a great deal of the tribal lands from financially strapped Indians, beginning in the Great Depression. St. Ignatius was far from cosmopolitan, but it presented an ethnic mix.

I stopped at a place called Yesterday's Cafe and got directions to Moose Lane, where Elwood Farmer lived. The counterman seemed surprised I had to ask; I might feel like an alien, but to his eyes I fit right in. He was white, and his gaze slid over me, then moved away in dismissal. Not a prejudiced look; to him I simply didn't count, and it made me wonder how many other such looks I'd received in my lifetime but never noticed. I glanced around at the half dozen diners seated in the shabby vinyl booths and realized with some shock that this was the first time I'd ever been in a room with so many people I resembled.

Moose Lane was off Second Street: narrow and unpaved, with small frame houses, many of which were flanked by what John called classic car collections. I followed it away from town through a pine forest that got denser with every tenth of a mile. Farmer's house sat in a clearing where the lane ended, a tidy log cabin with a new red pickup pulled in front of its porch and a plume of smoke drifting from a stovepipe chimney. I parked next to the truck and sat there for a moment, trying to trick myself into thinking this was a routine call on a witness who might provide useful information.

Sure it was.

*   *   *

The man who answered my knock was tall and muscular, with deep wrinkles on his nut-brown face and gray hair that hung to the shoulders of his plaid wool shirt. A cigarette was clamped between his lips. The nape of my neck prickled as I recognized a more masculine version of Mary McCone's chiseled features. A version of my own, too. His narrow eyes looked at me through the cigarette smoke, betraying nothing, not even curiosity. He cocked his head and waited for me to speak.

"Mr. Elwood Farmer?"

A slight nod.

"I'm Sharon McCone. My great-grandmother was your mother's sister."

Another nod, as if citified strangers often showed up on his porch, claiming kinship.

"May I talk with you, ask you some questions?"

He stepped out of the house, shut the door behind him. Removed the cigarette from his lips, dropped it on the floor, crushed it out. And waited.

I said, "My great-grandmother, Mary McCone, was Chief Tendoy's daughter by his third wife. She met my great-grandfather after she was kidnapped by an Indian agent, and went to California with him. I'm trying to trace my family's roots."

A long silence. Then, in a voice roughened not so much by age as tobacco and disuse, he asked, "Why?"

"Because . . . I need to know who I am."

A frown. Elwood Farmer drew in his lower lip, sucked thoughtfully on it.

"You don't know who you are?" he asked.

"Yes. No. I mean—"

He regarded me sternly. "Young woman, come back tomorrow, after you've assembled your thoughts."

Then he went inside and shut the door.

8:21 P.M.

"Assemble my thoughts," I muttered as I shifted position on the hard bed. "What the hell does that mean?"

My motel was on the northern end of town, twelve linoleum-floored units containing some of the ugliest and most uncomfortable furniture this side of Grand Rapids. Everything, even the remote control for the TV, was screwed down. I pressed the On button, flipped through the channels. Snow, snow, more snow, and a sitcom with a laugh track. Off!

After leaving Elwood Farmer's, I'd gone back to Yesterday's Cafe, had a bowl of chili, and asked for a recommendation of a place to stay. The man who waited on me this time was Native American; he took one look at my clothing and hairstyle and directed me to the AAA-endorsed motel. But they were full, so here I was. I folded my arms and stared glumly at a garish mountain landscape on the far wall.

I hadn't expected Elwood Farmer to welcome me with open arms; I was, after all, only a distant relative—if one at all. But I also hadn't expected to be greeted with silence and then a thinly veiled criticism of my mental processes. Maybe my blood relatives would turn out to be as weird as my adoptive family. Maybe I'd regret tracking them down.

One thing for sure, I'd regret spending any more time in this room than was absolutely necessary. I got up, combed my hair, grabbed my bag and jacket. Earlier I'd spotted a bar across the street, the Warbonnet Lounge; I'd go over there, have a drink, and assemble my thoughts—hopefully on a well-padded bar stool.

*   *   *

The Warbonnet Lounge was overly warm and smoke-clouded. No California-style outlawing of tobacco in drinking establishments here. A jukebox played country songs, and a few couples danced on the small floor in front of it. Danced with a Western flair like Hy did. Seeing them made me miss him, wish he'd been able to come along on this trip. But he was still at his ranch, working on a new project for his firm, and I was stuck in a small Montana town on a Friday night, where everybody seemed to be having a good time except me. I claimed one of the few unoccupied stools and ordered a draft.

Two men on my right were talking about cattle. On my left a couple were locked in such a torrid embrace that I felt like offering them the key to my motel room. After a few minutes they got up and wandered to the dance floor. Quickly the stool next to me was claimed by a thirties-ish man with thick raven hair and a silver hoop earring. He ordered a Coors, turned to me, and said, "You're the private detective from San Francisco."

"*What?*"

"Sharon McCone, the private detective who's related to Elwood Farmer."

"How do you—?"

He laughed with genuine pleasure. "Surprised? Maybe you should hire me, huh?"

". . . Maybe."

"You know, that stuff"—he motioned at my draft—"is terrible. Let me buy you a real beer."

I studied him. His narrow, elongated eyes gleamed mischievously; there was strength of character in the line of his jaw and good humor in the set of his mouth. This was someone I could like, and maybe develop as a contact within the reservation.

"Look," he added, "I'm not trying to hit on you. I've heard about you, is all, and I'm nosy."

"In that case, I'll take what you're having."

"You got it." He spoke to the bartender. "I'm Will Camphouse, by the way."

"And you already know who I am. How?"

"Moccasin telegraph."

"What's that?"

The bartender set down our beers, and Will Camphouse told him to run a tab. Then he looked around, spotted a booth opening up, and motioned toward it. After we were settled he said, "Okay, the moccasin telegraph. Indians communicate on it from coast to coast. Here's how it works: This afternoon Dwight Tendoy called his sister Millie Wasockie in Fort Hall and told her a descendant of Tendoy's missing daughter had surfaced and would probably come up here to talk with Elwood Farmer. Millie called her best friend, Candy Ferguson, in Arlee and asked if you'd arrived yet. Candy called Jane Nomee, here in Saint Ignatius, who called Elwood and confirmed the rumor. Moccasin telegraph."

Gossip central. "That doesn't explain how you know I'm from San Francisco, or a private investigator."

"Well, at the beginning of your conversation with Dwight Tendoy, you mentioned where you were calling from. So Jane Nomee asked her son Gilbert, who's a primo hacker, to find out more about you. He got a phone listing for your agency, plus some basic facts, and then he called his former college roommate, Keller Redbird, who lives in Frisco. Keller said he'd read about you in the papers, so Gilbert accessed some of the articles and printed them out. Jane took a set to Elwood, then got on the horn, and by now everybody in the original chain of information, plus their aunts, uncles, cousins, and dogs, knows about the private eye from the big city."

I shook my head. "I could use something like the moccasin telegraph in my business. But one thing still isn't clear: How'd you recognize me?"

"From a photo they printed with one of the articles. But I probably would've spotted you anyway; you're not dressed like most people on the rez." He pointed to the leather flight jacket that lay on the seat beside me.

"Neither are you." He wore an expensive-looking sweater, and when we sat down he'd shrugged out of a suede coat.

"Nope, I'm from Tucson. Creative director at an ad agency. Was born and raised there, but I visit the rez at least twice a year, once for my grandma's birthday—that's tomorrow—and for the Fourth of July powwow."

"Powwow? I thought that was something out of the movies, or strictly for tourists."

"Certainly not. Haven't you ever been to one?"

"No. What're they like?"

"Well, they're celebrations—our way of reinforcing our traditions. And they're a lot of fun: all sorts of traditional dances and games, tons of food, friends and relatives you haven't seen since the year before. The powwow makes you proud to be an Indian."

"I notice you say 'Indian,' rather than 'Native American.'"

"Most of us prefer 'Indian,' or our tribe's name. Or simply 'Native.' 'Native American' is mainly used by the media or academics or the politically correct. I've heard everything from 'Indigenous Americans' to 'Indigenous People' to 'Native American Indians.' But why speak a mouthful when one word'll do?" He paused, frowning. "You talk like an Angla. How the hell were you raised?"

"I'll explain that later. But first, what can you tell me

about Elwood Farmer? Dwight Tendoy described him as unusual."

"He is. Elwood was born and raised at Fort Hall; his mother was removed to there by the government after the old chief died. He got out early, though, went back East to art school. He's a good artist, made a lot of money in the white man's world when Indian art started to become chic with rich people. Met his wife Leila, a Saint Ignatius woman, in New York City. She was an artist too."

"And when did they move here?"

"In the late seventies. I don't know why. Elwood built his log house with his bare hands, but the day before they were to move in, Leila died in a car wreck. For a while Elwood went crazy—drank, fought, even tried to burn the house down. Then one day he sobered up completely. Started studying the traditional ways. Now he observes all the old Shoshone customs; does a lot of good for Indians throughout the state, too."

"How?"

"Travels around to the schools giving art workshops. He's a good teacher. The kids love him, really get off on the projects he assigns them. And it doesn't cost the schools a thing; he supplies the materials and teaches for free."

"He sounds like quite an impressive man." Farmer's example was interesting to me on a personal level: He'd tapped in to his Indian roots in middle age. Was it possible I could, too? Last spring I'd come to know a Hawaiian man whose life was deeply grounded in the ancient beliefs of his people, and I'd been totally baffled by what seemed to me a spooky, superstitious connection with the long-dead past. But now that I'd heard about Farmer's late awakening, I felt a stir of excitement.

Will looked at his watch. "Hey, I'd better get back to my

grandma's. She'll be thinking I've turned into a drunken injun."

The way he tossed off the offensive phrase made me frown.

"Look," he said, "when you've been pushed around as much as we have, you've gotta have a sense of humor. When I say stuff like that I'm really laughing at the white bigots who came up with it. So when're you going back to Elwood's?"

"Ah, you know about that too. First thing in the morning."

"Good. Tomorrow afternoon I want to take you someplace. And I want to hear your story."

"What story?"

"About why you talk and think like an Angla."

"I might be gone by then, Will."

He smiled and shook his head. "No, you won't."

"How come?"

"Trust me. I know Elwood Farmer."

Saturday

·

SEPTEMBER 9

10:55 A.M.

"And that's why I'm here."

I finished giving Elwood Farmer my account of the past week and waited for his response. We were sitting on a swing on the porch of his cabin, had been for most of an hour. The sun was taking the chill off the morning and raising my hopes of not losing a finger or a toe to frostbite.

Farmer smoked silently and contemplatively, as he had the whole time I talked. Finally he said, "Come back tomorrow."

"*What?*"

"Tomorrow morning, at nine."

He got up, went into the house, and shut the door.

3:15 P.M.

"So that's what I told Elwood," I said to Will Camphouse. "And then he ordered me to come back tomorrow and went in the house."

Will and I sat on a rocky outcropping on the west side of Flathead Lake, some seventy miles north of St. Ignatius. The sky had become overcast again, and the huge expanse of water lay placid and gray, highlighted occasionally as sun rays broke through the cloud cover. As I spoke I stared at the pine-covered hills on the far shore.

Will said, "I'm glad you agreed to drive up here this afternoon. I wanted you to see the lake, and I suspect you'll be leaving pretty soon. Elwood's almost ready to tell you what you need to know."

"If he is, he has a strange way of indicating it."

He shook his head. "Not really. He's been sizing you up, figuring out if he wants to befriend you. For us, friendship isn't defined by distant blood ties or physical proximity; it grows slowly through a series of interactions that test two people's mutual trust. But once a friendship's formed, it lasts forever."

"But you and I were friendly from the very first."

"That's different. I live in two worlds, move pretty easily from one to the other. For a lot of his life Elwood did too, so he'll come to a conclusion about you more quickly than most of the traditional people on the rez would."

"Three days is quick?"

"It can take months—years, even."

"Well, I can't spend my life here, going to see Elwood Farmer every day! I've got a business to run—"

"Relax. Like I said, he's about to tell you what you need to know."

"Who my parents were?"

"Maybe not that, but probably something about your great-aunt's visit to Fort Hall."

"It had to be Fort Hall, didn't it? Lemhi Valley was closed, and that was where Chief Tendoy's family were moved to.

Damn, if Elwood's going to talk, I wish he'd get on with it!"

"Impatient white-thinking woman."

We fell silent for a while. In spite of my frustration with Farmer's behavior, I felt at peace in this beautiful place, listening to the water lap at the rocks and the birds cry overhead. The vast Montana sky, which had seemed so oppressive only the day before, lifted my spirits; I felt a reassuring connectedness—to the water, the earth, the trees, the creatures that lived here. A connectedness to all people who loved such places and sought to preserve them.

Years ago, before I met Hy, I'd been a confirmed urbanite. Wide open spaces made me edgy, their silence drove me to distraction. But Hy, an environmental crusader, had flown me off to some of the most remote parts of the state: the White Mountains, the Trinity Alps, Death Valley. He'd shown me the comfort of their vastness, taught me to find peace in their silence.

"One thing, Sharon," Will said. "If Elwood tries to give you something, don't refuse it."

"What would he give me?"

"Oh, a photograph. Maybe a family treasure."

"I couldn't accept—"

"You have to. We're a people who love to give. Value or size doesn't matter, just the appropriateness of the gift for its recipient and the pleasure in sharing what we can. To refuse a gift is the greatest insult."

I sighed. "There's so much I don't understand."

"Inside, you know it all. Just let it come out slowly."

"You think that'll ever happen?"

"Sure. Let me ask you: D'you like to give?"

"I love to, much more than to receive. And I like to give gifts at any time, for no particular reason. If I see something that's perfect for somebody, I buy it and give it to them right away."

"There you go. Okay, what're your friendships based on?"

". . . A mutual trust, I guess. A sort of implied contract that it's give-and-take on either side. Sometimes I give the lion's share, sometimes the other person does, but over time it evens out. I'm cautious about accepting a person as a friend, but once I do, he or she is a friend for life."

"You see? It's all in the genes. Now let's head back to town. There're some people I want you to meet tonight."

8:05 P.M.

The people were his friends and family members, dozens of them of all ages. The place was a cousin's restaurant, and the occasion was his grandmother's seventieth birthday.

Long tables were laden with food: everything from chips and dip and fried chicken to dried deer meat and huckleberry tarts. Soft drinks and beer and wine were served, and nobody drank too much and became quarrelsome as we McCones had been known to do at family gatherings. Couples danced to loud music, children ran through the crowd, and everybody talked and laughed a lot. They all knew who I was and why I was there, so they accepted me with a cordial reserve.

As Will took me around and I sorted out names and faces, I began to pay particular attention to the women of my generation. They were lively, active, and spoke passionately of their work, families, and pursuits. Noreen was a partner with her husband in the bakery the tarts had come from; she freely admitted to having fallen victim to her own wares and talked of trying to expand the business and shrink her waistline. Gretchen, a Menominee from Wisconsin, ran a Headstart program and knowledgeably discussed grant writing with Emi, director of a youth-and-family-services agency. Violet was a weaver who talked with her hands as she described her line of capes, which were sold in specialty boutiques from coast to coast. Fran, a teacher, asked me what I thought of Elwood Farmer and spoke enthusiastically of the good he'd done her students. Janet was a writer who had put together an anthology of her tribe's oral history; she recited a brief story for me, and the words were like poetry.

As I listened to these women, I felt a kinship, coupled with a growing unease. They were very like my friends at home, and yet their issues—bicultural education, preservation of native traditions, eradication of alcoholism and spousal abuse—were not ones I'd had to face in the non-Indian world. As a white woman, an Angla, I'd dealt with mainstream issues, or often none at all. Now, if I were to find a place among my people, I'd be expected to identify with their concerns and move as easily from one world to another as they did. But could I do that?

No. It wasn't possible. Not yet, anyway, and maybe never. I felt trapped in a cultural no-man's-land, with no assurance of arriving safely at either border.

Sunday

•

SEPTEMBER 10

9:00 A.M.

"Come in, please," Elwood Farmer said.

I stepped into his small living room. It had a woodstove at its center and was furnished simply in pine and braided rugs; the walls were covered with framed pictures. Not Farmer's; judging from the childish technique of most, these had been done by his students. It fit with what I knew of the man that he would take little pride in his own work, but a great deal in that of the children he taught.

He motioned at one of two padded rockers facing the stove, and I sat. Lighting a cigarette, he took the other chair and scrutinized me for a moment through the smoke. I returned his gaze, expectant and nervous about what he had to tell me.

"You asked about Fenella McCone's visit to Fort Hall," he said. "That was in late summer of 1958."

Quick to the point, once he made up his mind to speak. "Did you meet her?"

"No. By then I had already moved to New York. You know I'm an artist?"

"Yes. And I know of your work in the schools. It's wonderful, what you're doing for the children."

He moved his hand as if to forestall further praise. "Most of the students aren't as fortunate as I was. My mother encouraged me, and later my work attracted the attention of a benefactor, a rich white New York woman who had a summer cabin on the Snake River and connections with a good art school." His lips twisted in amused memory. "She liked me, as well as my work. I guess I was good-looking back then, and I was certainly eager to please—in all areas."

So Elwood had his lively side. I smiled, and I could have sworn he winked at me—or maybe he was only blinking away smoke. "If you'd moved away, how do you know about my aunt's visit?"

"I believe my nephew has told you of the moccasin telegraph."

"Will Camphouse is your nephew?"

"In a distant way. Our familial relationships aren't as clear-cut as whites', or as formal."

"Does that mean he's related to me too?"

". . . Possibly. There's been so much mixing among the tribes, and other ethnic groups as well, that those connections are very difficult to sort out. If you and Will want to be related, then you should consider yourselves so."

His words opened up a startling and somewhat alarming array of possibilities. I pictured myself surrounded by circles of people, all of them strangers and each potential kin. While I wasn't exactly a loner, I kept my own family at arm's length and my close friends were limited to fewer than a dozen. Now, by virtue of blood, any number of people might be able to lay claim to me.

I said, "About Fenella . . ."

"She was the big news story on the moccasin telegraph

that year. Remember, this was the nineteen-fifties. It wasn't common for women to appear alone in sports cars and descend on relatives who, up till then, hadn't been aware of their existence. And your great-aunt was very exotic."

"Fenella, exotic?" It wasn't a term I'd ever associated with her.

"Oh, yes." Farmer nodded. "She looked Irish, with all that red hair and pale skin. The hair was dyed, the women said. She wore shorts and halter tops that showed off her figure, and usually went barefoot. The men followed her around like puppy dogs, but the women took to her too. They said there wasn't any meanness in her. She was natural and friendly and cared deeply about her roots and our people. She was generous, and she laughed at herself, rather than others."

"You speak as if you knew Fenella well, but you say you never met her."

"I didn't, but I feel as though I had. That year I returned to the reserve for Christmas, stayed into January. Talk of your great-aunt was rekindled when she sent presents, as well as two big crates of Florida oranges."

"What did Fenella do on the reservation?"

"Mainly what my students call hanging out. She got the women to teach her the rudiments of some of our crafts, and she spent time with an elder who was a storyteller, learning about the legends and history. She took the younger people off on trips in her sports car, just piled them in and drove away. After six weeks she left, but she kept in touch by letter and sent presents till she died."

So there might be some correspondence in that box John had found at Pa's.

"Let me show you something," Elwood Farmer said. He went to a bookcase where some framed photographs sat and brought one to me. The frame was bleached bone, carved to resemble buffalo moving nose to tail, and its contours were worn smooth by the passage of many fingers. I looked questioningly at Farmer.

"My father made it from the last scraps of buffalo bone that my mother's father saved after the white man decimated the herds." The sorrow in his voice was as great as if he had been of the generations who hunted the bison and used its body for food, clothing, shelter, tools, and weapons.

I looked down at the grainy black-and-white photograph: a group of six people, with Fenella at the center. My great-aunt smiled for the camera, clad in tight shorts and an off-the-shoulder peasant blouse, her eyes masked by big harlequin-style sunglasses. Her companions were four more conservatively attired Indian women, probably in their teens, and a slightly older white man, whose face was shaded by a cowboy hat.

"Who are these people?" I asked.

"Young women from the reservation." He pointed them out. "Lucy Edmo, Barbara Teton, Susan New Moon, Saskia Hunter."

"And the man?"

". . . I don't know. Could be a visitor like your great-aunt."

"From the way they're smiling, they look as if they're all good friends."

"They were."

I studied the photo's background, a stucco building with a sign, but I couldn't make out what it said. "Where was this taken?"

"The old trading post in Fort Hall. It's gone now, replaced by a mini-mart."

I nodded and set the photograph on the table between

our chairs. So much was gone now, maybe even all these people. "D'you know where I might reach the women in the picture?"

He shook his head, eyes turning bleak. I sensed one of the women had meant something to him, and that was why he'd kept the picture in the special frame all these years.

"Can you think of anyone who might be able to tell me more about Fenella's visit?"

"Well, there's Agnes Running Horse, my cousin. She lives on the Middle Fork of the Flathead River near Glacier National Park."

"Would she be willing to talk with me?"

Something moved under the surface of his gaze, a deep, dark current that I couldn't define. "I'm sure she will."

"How far away is her place?"

"A hundred miles, give or take, but the roads aren't fast ones. Still, you could be there this afternoon."

"Will you call her and tell her who I am and that I'm coming?"

He nodded, took a pad from the table and scribbled directions.

When I stood to go, I said, "Mr. Farmer, thank you so much."

"No thanks are necessary. But I hope—"

"Yes?"

He shook his head, dismissing whatever he'd been about to say. "I want to give you something." He picked up the photograph from the table, caressed its frame gently, then pressed it into my hands.

My first instinct was to refuse such a precious gift, but then I remembered Will Camphouse's caution against giving offense, and instead caressed the frame as Farmer had. "I'm honored," I said. "I'll treasure it always."

The dark current in his eyes moved more strongly. "I hope so, my friend. Travel safely."

11:48 A.M.

"What did Elwood give you?" Will Camphouse asked me.

"How d'you know that he did?"

"I just know."

"Well, you're right." I slipped the framed photograph from my bag and showed it to him. He whistled softly.

"I guess it means he thinks I'm okay," I said.

"More than okay. He's accepted you as family."

"D'you know any of these people in the picture?"

He shook his head. "I've seen it at Elwood's place, though. I don't know which he treasures more—the photo or the frame."

"I don't know either."

We were seated at a weathered picnic table in the park across from Yesterday's Cafe, eating deli sandwiches. The overcast continued, and the wind had picked up; it blew trash from a nearby barrel and sent it dancing over the packed earth.

I said, "Speaking of family, Elwood claims you and I might be related."

"We probably are. Bloodlines're kind of tangled in the Indian world."

"Frankly, I'm sick of thinking about bloodlines. For forty years I knew exactly who I was. Now . . ."

"You'll sort it out."

"How can you say that when you yourself don't know who's a relation and who's not?"

"Well, maybe you'll decide it's not important."

"What can be more important than your own identity?"

"Maybe you'll figure that out too."

I narrowed my eyes at him. "Being enigmatic today, are we?"

He grinned.

"Well, I'm glad we might be related," I said. "And I'm glad I ran into you at the Warbonnet."

"No accident there. Elwood sent me to track you down and report on you."

"But how'd you know where to find me?"

"Easy, in a town this size. I knew what motel you were staying at, because the owner had put the word out. And what's near that motel? A gas station, two dead businesses, an auto-body shop, and the Warbonnet."

"Maybe I *should* hire you."

"If I ever get sick of the ad biz, I'll give you a call."

We'd finished our sandwiches, and now I looked at my watch. "I should get going. Agnes Running Horse is expecting me."

"You'll like her. She's seventy-nine, going on thirty."

Suddenly I was reluctant to leave this maybe-relative who had shown me so much kindness. "You've got my card. You'll keep in touch?"

"Uh-huh. And you've got my card too."

I balled up the wrapper from my sandwich, tossed it in the trash barrel, and continued to sit there.

"Hey," Will said, "I know what you might find out is scary, but you'd better get on with it." When I didn't reply, he jerked his chin at my rental car. "Go. Now!"

I smiled and stood, started walking away. Then Will called, "Hey, catch!"

I turned, put my hands out for the small, flat cardboard box that was flying toward me. "What . . . ?"

"Open it tonight, wherever today takes you. And not a minute before."

3:45 P.M.

Agnes Running Horse and I walked along the bank of the Flathead River across the highway from where her brown frame house nestled under a towering wooded ledge. The air was crisp and colder up here near Glacier, and the only sounds were the ripple of water as it flowed around the off-shore rocks, the occasional swoosh of tires on the pavement, and the crunch of gravel under our feet. Mrs. Running Horse—a small, spry woman with a long gray ponytail and deep laugh lines around her eyes—had met me at her door and explained that this was the time she customarily took her daily walk.

"Yeah," she told me now, "your great-aunt was the way Elwood said. I liked her, even if she couldn't do beadwork for shit." When I glanced at her in surprise, she grinned. "I'm old. I can talk as dirty as I want. Believe me, that Fenella had a mouth on her. Tendoys do."

"So she told you who her mother was. When I spoke with Dwight Tendoy, he said nobody knew what happened to Mary."

"Not many did, but that Fenella had to explain herself. She told me and a couple of the other women, asked us not to spread it around. Her mother only talked about the family and the past once—because Fenella said she had a right to know—and she wasn't happy with her for looking up the relatives."

"Why, d'you suppose?"

Mrs. Running Horse motioned at a concrete abutment

alongside a boat-launching ramp, and we sat. The river was narrow here, lodgepole pine and scrub vegetation crowding down the hills to the opposite bank. At its bend I could see the peaks of the national park, bluish in the haze.

"I suppose," she said, "Mary wanted to forget those times because they were so tough. Even after they moved from Lemhi Valley to Fort Hall, the government was chintzy with them. Chief Tendoy was dead, and none of his sons could get action out of Washington. Then there was that bastard agent, John Blaine: When the allotments did come, he took the best for himself and sold it. Took Mary, too. Dragged her down to Arizona, beat her, got her pregnant. Left her."

"She had a child?"

"It died at birth. She almost died too. She was starving on the trail outside of Flagstaff when your great-grandfather came through, and plenty glad to go with him. Fenella said Mary blamed her brothers for not rescuing her from Blaine, so she turned her back on the family."

I didn't remember my great-grandmother, but her picture had sat on a table in our living room: stern and stiffly posed, a simple gold cross the only ornamentation against her plain black dress. Religion, family, womanly duties—they were the walls she'd built against the memory of privation, abuse, and abandonment. I felt a wave of pity, both for the mistreated teenager and the immured adult.

"Is there anything else you want to ask me?" Agnes Running Horse said.

I reached into my bag for the photograph Elwood Farmer had given me. "Can you tell me who this man is, and where I might find these women?"

She examined it for a long time, tapping her fingers on the frame. "Where'd you get this?"

"From Mr. Farmer. He named the women, but he didn't know the man."

"Yes—Lucy Edmo, Barbara Teton, Susan New Moon, Saskia Hunter. Barbara's dead, breast cancer. Everybody thought Elwood would marry her, but they had a big fight the last time he came home to the reserve, and that was it. Saskia Hunter, I heard she went to college, made something of herself, but I don't know what. I'm surprised Elwood couldn't tell you; they were real good friends. The other two, I don't know."

She paused, looking reflectively at the photo. "Nobody stays in one place anymore. Even me: I came up here from Fort Hall twenty-seven years ago to take care of my son and his kids when his wife died. Thought it'd be just for a year or two till he found a new wife, but he never did, and I never went home. Now *he's* dead, the kids're scattered, and I'm getting old enough to start thinking about going to live with my daughter in Kalispell."

I glanced at her, saw her face was free of sadness or regret. Those were simply the facts and, if anything, she was not displeased with how her life had turned out.

"The man in the picture," I said. "Are you sure you don't know him?"

". . . I don't know his name. Those days, there were a lot of white boys drifting around the country. They'd read that Kerouac, wanted to be beatniks, or whatever they called them. Usually kids whose parents had more money than good sense. They'd show up on the reserve, take up with a girl, then disappear."

"This man, he's standing next to Saskia Hunter. Is she the one he took up with?"

"Yes."

"And then he disappeared?"

". . . Yes."

"And you say you don't know what happened to her, other than she went to college?"

"That's right."

"Can you think of anyone else I might contact regarding Fenella's visit to Fort Hall?"

She shook her head, eyes fixed on the distant peaks. "I'm sorry, but at my age you get forgetful. Lose track of people, too, when they scatter to the cities. That visit was so very long ago."

So very long ago, yet still such a strong force upon my present.

11:51 P.M.

By the time I got to the airport in Missoula, the last San Francisco flight had long departed. As always when stranded in transit, I opted for motion and boarded a 747 for Seattle. Once we were airborne, I decided this was the place where today had taken me and opened Will Camphouse's gift.

It was a small circle covered in pale beige skin. A web of delicate threads bisected its interior, each with a turquoise bead knotted into it. Three white feathers were secured to its bottom by silver-and-turquoise clamps. A note from Will accompanied it:

It's called a dreamcatcher, and here's how it works: you put it over your bed, or wherever you crash in your travels, and it catches the bad dreams but lets the good ones through. It's the best gift I could think of for you,

because you'll probably need it in the nights to come.
So sleep well, friend. My thoughts are with you.

I fingered the soft feathers of the dreamcatcher, then
placed it on the empty seat beside me. Maybe it would fend
off the demons of the night.

LISTENING . . .

There're a few silences in today's conversations. Wonder
if I can interpret them. It's not all that easy with people I've
known all my life, and Elwood Farmer and Agnes Running
Horse are strangers from a different culture.

"Who are these people?"
*"Young women from the reservation. Lucy Edmo, Barbara
Teton, Susan New Moon, Saskia Hunter."*
"And the man?"
". . . I don't know. Could be a visitor like your great-aunt."

What's Elwood thinking of when he hesitates? Picture his
eyes, filtered as they are through the smoke from his cigarette.

At first they're uncertain, but then they harden. He's made
a decision and he's sticking to it. What?

Not to tell me who the man is, even though he knows? Why would that be?

"*Mr. Farmer, thank you so much.*"
"*No thanks are necessary. But I hope—*"

Why doesn't he finish the sentence? What does he hope? And what does that dark stirring in his gaze mean? Sadness there, distress too. Is he concerned for me, or for himself? Or for someone else entirely?

"*The man in the picture. Are you sure you don't know him?*"
"*. . . I don't know his name. Those days, there were a lot of white boys drifting around the country.*"

Agnes Running Horse isn't a very good liar. Like Elwood, she knows who the man is, but for some reason she doesn't want to say. Why not?

"*This man, he's standing next to Saskia Hunter. Is she the one he took up with?*"
"*Yes.*"
"*And then he disappeared?*"
"*. . . Yes.*"

Another hesitation. This time she's looking away at the mountain peaks, avoiding my eyes. The man didn't disappear, at least not the same way other young men who'd gone on the road and ended up on the reservation had. That's why Mrs. Running Horse doesn't want to name him.

She was forthcoming and lively when she talked about Mary McCone. It wasn't till she saw the picture that she became reticent. The way she looked at it: there was pain in her eyes, but not for herself; she isn't a woman who indulges in self-pity. No, the pain was for someone else.

That picture. Why did Elwood Farmer give it to me? He could easily have offered a lesser gift. Unless he thought it important that I have it. Unless he considered it central to my search. . . .

Monday

•

SEPTEMBER 11

12:14 A.M.

I took the photograph from my bag, turned on the reading light over my seat, and stared at it as if willing the people frozen in the frame to confide their secrets to me. Even Fenella seemed to be hiding behind her big sunglasses. The photo was not a very good one, the contrast curiously muted. Not taken by a good photographer or with a good camera. Or . . .

I held it up to the light, examined it more carefully. Then I turned it over, bent the metal clips that held it in the frame, removed the backing.

Slick paper with printing on the back. It wasn't an original photo, but a clipping from a magazine. The dateline at the bottom of the page said *Newsweek*, February 13, 1959.

I removed the clipping and turned it over to see if there was a caption for the picture that the frame had covered. It looked as if it had been cut off. Was *Newsweek* online? Did the available issues go back that far? Maybe.

There was a phone in the seatback. I took out a credit card, ran it through, dialed Mick and Charlotte's condo.

Keim answered, sounding groggy. When I identified myself and asked for Mick, she said, "Shar, you're pure hell on a gal's beauty sleep," and covered the receiver. Soon after, Mick growled into it.

"I know it's late," I said, "but consider this a challenge."

Yawn.

"I need an article from the February 13, 1959, issue of *Newsweek*." I described the photograph, told him what was on the back of it.

"I think I can get hold of it. Where can I reach you?"

"You can't, but I'll call you when I get to Seattle."

"Why Seattle?"

"It seemed as good a place as any."

"The picture you wanted," Mick said, "was printed with an article about how well off the Indians were on the reservations. What was Fenella doing there?"

"Trying to find her roots, like me. Does the caption identify the man?"

"Yeah, I'll read it to you. 'Happy Fort Hall dwellers with outside friends, Fenella McCone, who is half Shoshone, and Austin DeCarlo, son of a prominent central California rancher.'"

"Any mention of him in the article?"

"Nope. Shar, this piece is a bunch of bull. I've been to reservations, and they're not great places. I bet they were worse in the fifties."

"Lots worse, according to the file you prepared for me. It's a puff piece, that's all."

"You in Seattle?"

"Yes, but not for long. I called a pilot buddy who's always ready to fly, and she agreed to take me home for the price of fuel and breakfast."

"Why don't I fax the article to your house, then?"

"Do that. And first thing in the morning, start a check on Austin DeCarlo."

The box of Fenella's papers that John had FedExed sat just inside my front door, along with a package containing some jeans I'd ordered from Lands' End. Michelle Curley, neighbor kid and house-sitter extraordinaire, was being conscientious again. I paid her twenty-five dollars a month to take care of the cats when I wasn't home, plus check for mail and deliveries. She earned every cent of it and often exceeded her job description: when I'd come home from San Diego, the dishes were washed and flowers from her parents' garden brightened my sitting room.

I left the Lands' End bag where it was, but dragged the box down the hall. Tore the article Mick had faxed from the machine in my home office, then set the coffeemaker to brewing, in spite of already having downed three cups during an airport breakfast with my pilot friend. While the machine burbled, I took a quick shower and read the article while I dried my hair. A puff piece, all right. I particularly disliked the concluding paragraphs.

Our federal government's termination of ties to the reservation system has indeed, in the words of Senator Arthur Watkins (R-Utah), "emancipated the Indian." Statutes calling for the preparation of final tribal rolls, distribution of assets to individuals, and the removal of Indian lands from federal trusts will give natives increased independence and self-determination.

Already this new era in reservation life is producing positive results: Interest in traditional crafts and religion is surging; tourism is at an all-time high; tribe members are looking forward to a bright and fulfilling future. No wonder our team of reporters encountered so much joy and optimism as they traveled the country last summer visiting these havens of native culture.

Joy and optimism, my ass! I had enough of a sense of history to know that the Indians had seldom had occasion for either, before or after termination. While under the auspices of the federal government, they'd waited desperately for food, clothing, and medical supplies that arrived late or not at all. They'd lived in substandard housing, been forced to convert to Christianity by missionaries of every stripe, and had their children snatched from their homes and shipped off to boarding schools designed to eradicate every trace of their traditional culture.

And then, in the 1940s and '50s, came termination. The Indians found themselves "emancipated," all right—of their access to the Indian Health Service and educational assistance programs. Their lands became subject to state taxation, and many tribe members were forced to sell to outsiders. State laws were extended to their territories, and they lost the right to police their own communities. The "joyful and optimistic" Indians watched their lives plunge into a downward spiral of poor health, illiteracy, and poverty.

Admittedly, the Shoshones in the photograph with Fenella looked happy, but I doubted it had anything to do with the "new era" on the rez. More likely they were just having a good time together and mugging for the photographer— perhaps laughing at the white men who had come there with their minds already made up about what they'd find.

* * *

Back in the kitchen, I realized it was going to be one of those Mondays. The coffeemaker had sprung a leak and grounds puddled the countertop. The fridge was making a familiar grinding sound, signaling that I'd soon need a new one. One of the cats—or maybe both—had attacked the garlic braid hanging from a cabinet. And now they emerged from wherever they'd been sleeping, eager for breakfast.

"Right," I said, regarding them sternly, "the human can-and-door-opener is home."

Allie gave me one of her adoring looks; Ralph brushed against my calves, purring. Were they strictly con artists, or actually glad to see me? I'd never know.

The livestock fed, watered, and put out to pasture, I took my coffee to the sitting room and used a paring knife to cut the yards of tape that John—who is sure the contents of any package he wraps are seriously intent on escape—had swathed it in. When I raised the lid, all that made a break for it was musty air, the smell of paper stored too long in a damp garage. I dumped out the contents and began sorting them.

A sentimental fool Fenella hadn't been. There were no letters, photographs, or mementos. Just a great many legal documents, receipts, canceled checks, and bank statements, going back to about twenty years before her death. Again, my pack-rat father had kept the unnecessary.

At first I was tempted to toss everything into the fireplace, but then I decided to go through it anyway. A will, dividing her property between Pa and Jim. Lease on an apartment she'd rented in San Diego. High school and college diplomas. Well-worn passport. Charge-account receipts. Pay stubs from her various jobs as a bookkeeper. Checks:

to the grocery, the dry cleaner, the landlord, the phone company, PG&E, and—

Saskia Hunter.

A check made out in the amount of $2,500. August of 1962. A considerable sum in those days.

I began pawing through the other checks, came up with a total of fifteen made out to Hunter, beginning in December of 1959 and each in the same amount. All were dated in either August or December, the last in December of 1966.

There was a stack of bank statements accompanying the checks. I took them to the kitchen table, poured myself more coffee, and studied the pattern of deposits. Many matched the pay stubs, but others were larger; that didn't surprise me, since the family had always suspected Fenella of allowing her gentlemen friends to supplement her income. But several of these larger deposits stood out: in July and November of every year from 1960 to 1966, her account was credited with $2,500—which she'd turned over to Saskia Hunter a month later.

I picked up the photograph in the buffalo-bone frame and studied Hunter. Then I closed my eyes and pictured the photograph of Mary McCone that had sat in my family's living room. Yes, what they said was true: I bore a strong resemblance to her. But I bore an even stronger one to Saskia Hunter.

My scalp prickled and I narrowed my eyes, trying to make out the features of the man next to Hunter. The wide brim of his cowboy hat shadowed them, made them difficult to define. He had a strong jaw and full lips, but that was all I could tell.

Well, I had a name for him—Austin DeCarlo—and soon Mick would start his trace. Right now I'd start my trace on Hunter.

*   *   *

D.O.B. April 4, 1941, Fort Hall, Idaho. She'd been seventeen when the *Newsweek* photo was taken. Parents: Harry and Rose Tendoy Hunter, both deceased. One of the relatives Fenella had found, then.

No record of a marriage in Bingham County. No death certificate, either. No phone listing.

Two public high schools in the vicinity. I called one and asked for the school librarian; she pulled the yearbook for 1958. Saskia Hunter had graduated in the top half of her class, and the write-up below her picture said she hoped to become a teacher.

Any record of where she had attended college? I asked. The librarian transferred me to the guidance counselor. She told me their records for the fifties were in storage.

There were a number of Hunters in the area phone directory. I started calling.

"Strange name, Saskia. If we were related, I'd remember it."

"Never heard of her."

"My wife and me, we just moved to Idaho."

"Lady, in case you don't realize it, Hunter is a common name."

"I knew a Kia Hunter in high school. Don't know what happened to her."

"Kia and I are related, sort of. But I lost track of her a long time ago."

"Miss, I got three screaming kids and I'm baby-sitting my sister's mutt. This isn't the time to be asking me stupid questions."

End of list. Dead end. Now what?

The phone rang. Mick. "Here's the preliminary information on Austin DeCarlo," he said. "D.O.B. 11/22/36, Salinas. Parents: Audrey Simms and Joseph DeCarlo. Mother, housewife; father, rancher. The mother's deceased, father still lives on the ranch near King City. It was a working cattle ranch till 1980, now most of it's in vineyards. Austin DeCarlo owns a home in Monterey, where he has his corporate offices."

"What kind of corporation?"

"Real estate development. DeCarlo Enterprises. They build luxury resorts. I downloaded info from their Web site."

"Any further personal details?"

"Two marriages: Dawn Chase, in King City, 1961. Divorced 1970, no children. Anna Bastoni, in Monterey, 1971. Divorced 1989, no children."

"Education?"

"Graduated King City High, 1953. Attended Cal Poly from 'fifty-three to 'fifty-six, no degree. That's all I've got so far. I'll fax this over to you, and keep working on it."

"Thanks, Mick."

"You're welcome. By the way, you didn't tell me what file to allocate my time to."

"None, for now. Just keep track of the hours."

"Ted's not gonna like that. You've been gone so much lately that he's picking more nits than usual."

And that would be a great many nits indeed. "If he gives you any trouble, tell him to talk to me."

The material Mick faxed gave the addresses of Austin DeCarlo's home and office in Monterey, as well as of his father's ranch. I dragged out my California road map and consulted it, then studied an aviation sectional for the area. It would be a quick trip by plane, but Hy had Two-seven-Tango at Tufa Lake. I supposed I could rent one, but on top of that expense I'd have the cost of a car once I got there. Besides, the lure of the open road was strong; it had been a long time since my venerable MG and I had headed south on Highway 101. I made a few calls, repacked my travel bag, and soon we were on our way.

The San Francisco Peninsula: small cities strung together, mostly indistinguishable from one another. If we didn't check the current rate of development, California would be one border-to-border city in fifty years. San Jose: a growing metropolis that reminded me of L.A., both in sprawl and smog. Salinas: writer John Steinbeck's hometown, and a much better place now that they'd finally decided to honor their most renowned native son. Westward on the back road from there, toward Highway 1 and Monterey.

And, maybe, Austin DeCarlo.

1:15 P.M.

The sky was clear over the cobalt expanse of Monterey Bay, where the shoreline's protective arc makes for some of the best weather along the central coast. I drove south on Lighthouse Avenue, the wide commercial boulevard on the hill above Steinbeck's fabled Cannery Row, looking for my side street.

Mick's information on Austin DeCarlo was sketchy enough that I couldn't come up with a plan on how to approach him. Taking a look at both his home and offices seemed like a good first step; then I'd phone my nephew and ask if he'd found any further details. I made a quick left turn in front of a slow-moving van and climbed uphill to Archer Street.

DeCarlo's house was on the northeast side: white clapboard, three stories, with many windows. A huge semicircle of glass took up most of the front wall of the third story, and there was probably an identical one opposite to take advantage of the bay view. The house was an older one, and the more modern top floor didn't fit—a remodeling job whose architect had seen the parts, rather than the whole.

As I pulled to the curb and idled there, the garage door rose and a woman came out: thin, with bleached and permed hair, dressed in baggy jeans and an oversized T-shirt imprinted with a sea otter. I shut the MG off, got out, and approached her. She pushed an interior button and stepped aside as the door started to close.

"Excuse me," I said. "Is Mr. DeCarlo at home?"

She frowned and started to walk away. I took out my ID folder and flashed my license at her, just long enough that she could see it looked official. "Tax inquiry. I need to speak with him."

The words erased the crease between her eyebrows, and a sly expression crept over her face. She stopped, shifting a plastic sack containing a bottle of cleaning solvent and some rags from one hand to the other. DeCarlo's maid, and she didn't seem at all sorry that the boss might be about to get audited.

"He's not here," she said.

"Is he at the office?"

"No, out of town. Last week he tells me come in and clean like always. And then he didn't leave my money."

"That's too bad. D'you know where he went?"

"Uh-uh."

"Or when he'll be back?"

"Who knows, with him? Maybe tonight, maybe next week. He travels a lot, but this is the first time he forgot my money." She sighed, looking up and down the street as if she hoped to spot her employer. "I was counting on it. Now I don't even have my bus fare back to Sand City."

Opportunity was fairly pounding on my door. "How much does he owe you?"

"Fifty dollars. Doesn't sound like much, but I really need it."

"How about if I give you the fifty? And drive you to Sand City?"

"What's in it for you? You want me to rat him out?"

I smiled.

"Let's go," she said.

Terry—"No last name, I don't want to lose my job"— didn't like her employer. As we drove north on the freeway, she made that abundantly clear.

Austin DeCarlo was too rich for his own good: "All that stuff. Sound systems, TVs in every room, indoor hot tub, big wine cellar, boat, fancy cars. He *must* be cheating the government."

Every week he left the house in a "god-awful mess": "He wants to cook, he oughta clean up the pots and pans and the grease on the stove. Newspapers and magazines don't belong on the floor. Dirty dishes, hairs in the bathroom sink. And I can't respect a man who won't hang up his expensive clothes."

He behaved in an unseemly fashion for one of his age: "Women. Different ones. Young ones. All the time. And he's gotta be pushing sixty. Disgusting!"

DeCarlo was rude, too: "He yells at me if I start vacuuming while he's on the phone."

Even his choice of pets was unfortunate: "Big dog. Irish setter. Goes everyplace with him. Leaves its hairs everyplace for me to clean up. Man treats that dog better than he treats most people! Hey, that's my exit up ahead."

"Anything else you can tell me about him?" I asked as I put on the turn signal.

"Not really. I mean, it's not like I saw his tax forms or anything. But I'm sure he's a cheater."

"Why?"

"Well, he's trying to cheat those Indians, so why wouldn't he cheat the IRS too?"

"What Indians?"

"Up north someplace. My old boyfriend Chuck told me. He's got Indian blood, and he said old Austin's trying to cheat them. The Indians."

"How?"

"Something about putting a resort on their land. I can't remember anything more about it."

"Can you put me in touch with Chuck?"

"Nope, he's history. Moved away two months ago."

"You sure you don't remember anything else?"

"Uh . . . a name, maybe. Ghost? Nope, that's not it. Spirit? Yeah, Spirit something."

"*What* something?"

"Can't remember. Hey, drop me here, would you? I don't want you knowing where I live."

Spirit.

The word had a familiar ring in connection with Austin DeCarlo. Maybe it was mentioned in the material Mick had supplied on DeCarlo Enterprises. I pulled the MG into the

parking lot of a strip mall and took the file from the brief-
case in the carrying space behind me.

The company's Web site described it as the leading de-
veloper of exclusive resorts in the United States: Saguaro in
Santa Fe; Blue Glacier in Homer, Alaska; Merlot in the Napa
Valley; Mountain High outside of Boulder, Colorado; The
Breakers in Neskowin, Oregon. And those were just the ones
I'd heard of. Photographs showed impressive architecture,
golf courses, swimming pools, restaurants, and guest bun-
galows. Projects were currently under construction or in the
planning stages on the Hawaiian island of Lanai and St.
Thomas in the U.S. Virgin Islands; in Sedona, Arizona, and
Modoc County, California.

Up north someplace. Well, Modac County was about as
far north as you could get in the state, tucked up in the
corner against the Oregon and Nevada borders. I'd never
been there, and its only town of any size that I knew of was
Alturas, whose population couldn't be more than a few
thousand.

I reached for the side pocket where I kept my AAA guide,
paged to the listing. Right, there were 4,300 people in Alturas. Formerly called Dorris Bridge after the first white set-
tler, it was the Modoc County seat and a marketing center
for local ranchers. Its sole tourist attraction was a histori-
cal museum, and the guide recommended two motels, no
restaurants.

I exchanged the guide for my state *Thomas Guide.* The
majority of the county was national forest, tiny towns, and
reservoirs. A large lake—Goose—extended north over the
Oregon border, and there were a number of smaller lakes
and rivers. Highway 395—which, if taken south, would
eventually lead to Tufa Lake, near Hy's ranch—bisected the

county. To the east the Warner Mountains rose as high as 9,000 feet.

Spirit something. I scanned the map in segments, finally found it: Spirit Lake, near a small settlement called Sage Rock. A remote place for a resort, but not if you were aiming at the high-end traveler who valued isolation and privacy. Put in a world-class restaurant and golf course, an airstrip capable of accommodating good-size jets, and you'd be in business.

But the lake wasn't on an Indian reservation, or even near one. How could Austin DeCarlo be trying to cheat anyone?

I took out my phone and called Mick at the office. Ted, sounding annoyed, said he'd assigned him to call on a new client. "Whatever you've got him working on is cutting into our billable hours," he complained.

"Let me worry about that."

"You ought to worry. We're looking at a rent increase come spring, and do you know what the last PG and E bill was? When're you going to be back in the office?"

"I'm not sure."

"So in the meantime I'm supposed to hold everything together."

"I trust you to do that, yes."

A long silence. "Oh, hell, I'm worried about you, is all. You haven't been yourself since your dad died."

He didn't know the half of it. "Thanks for your concern. Can you hang in there a little longer?"

"I'll hang in however long you need. Do you want me to tell Mick to call you?"

"No." I gave him the details of what Mick should search for and asked him to pass them along. Ted was a good friend, a good employee, and—although he didn't know it yet—I had big plans for his future.

4:05 P.M.

The land southeast of King City was softly contoured, hillocks of sunburnt grass where brown-and-white-faced cattle grazed. This was old ranching country, not much changed from the turn of the century when little valley towns such as San Ardo and Bradley were centers of commerce for people off the big spreads and small farms. I'd even passed a dilapidated barn with a still-readable advertisement for Mail Pouch Tobacco on its wall.

The DeCarlo ranch was on Cat Canyon Road, some dozen miles into the country; the dry brown grass gave way to vineyards where row after row of plants were beginning to show fall color. A hopper truck full of grapes was turning onto the road from a driveway, and I had to swing wide to avoid it. Harvesttime in the Salinas Valley.

The gate across the drive stood open, so I turned in and followed the blacktop to a cluster of metal sheds where workers, mostly Hispanic, milled about. A tall gray-haired man in Levi's and a Western-style shirt was waving for another truck to leave. I pulled the MG to one side and got out.

As the truck departed, the tall man noticed me and started over. He was very lean, the Levi's loose and riding low on his hips, and his unruly mane of hair gleamed in the sun. The furrows on his rawhide-tanned face told me he must be over eighty—a hearty eighty, though. Years of activity out in the elements had bred toughness and kept an agile spring in his step.

"Hello!" I called. "I'm looking for Joseph DeCarlo."

He slowed, his demeanor wary now. "What d'you want with him?"

"To talk about a personal matter. Is he on the ranch today?"

The man stopped in front of me, his faded blue eyes squinting down at my face. He made a motion to the men behind him, and they dispersed silently and quickly—all except one, a stocky, powerfully muscled Hispanic who stood with folded arms, leaning against a pickup truck.

I said, "My name's Sharon McCone," and held out one of my cards.

The man nodded as if he'd known that all along. He took the card but didn't read it, still studying me. "Son of a bitch," he said. "You even look like her."

"Like who?"

"As if you didn't know. She send you?"

"I don't understand what you're talking about. I'm a private investigator, here on a confidential inquiry."

He glanced at my card, then threw his head back and gave a harsh bark of laughter. "Now don't that just tear it! Did some snooping on your own, and you liked what you found out. Well, let me tell you this, missy: I've had a lot of years to think on the subject. A lot of time to plan for the day this might happen. So here's what you're gonna do: get off my ranch and leave my boy alone."

His ranch. "You're Joseph DeCarlo."

"You know who I am."

"I'd like to speak with you. And with your son."

"I'll bet you would. Trouble is, my boy and I don't want to speak with *you.*"

"Why don't we let your son decide for himself?"

"No, missy, that's not how it works around here."

"How *does* it work?"

DeCarlo stepped forward, looming over me. "It works the way I say it should." He snapped his fingers, and the man leaning on the pickup came over. "This is Tony. He's head of ranch security. He's gonna escort you off my property—politely. You come back, he won't be near as polite."

Tony went to the MG, opened the driver's door, and motioned for me to get in. I ignored him.

"Mr. DeCarlo, your 'boy' is a grown man in his sixties. D'you really think he wants his father dictating who he can and can't speak to?"

"He does what I tell him to."

"Always?"

His lips twitched; I'd hit a nerve. He motioned to the security man, who came over and took my arm.

I said, "I've an idea that your son might be interested in talking with me about Fort Hall, Idaho. And Saskia Hunter."

Joseph DeCarlo's face reddened. He said to Tony, "Get her out of here!"

Tony tried to take my arm, but I pushed him aside. Then I took my time about getting into the MG and driving away.

When I got to the road I turned left, rather than back the way I'd come. The pavement curved to the southeast, following the perimeter of the DeCarlo property. After nearly a mile I spotted another driveway and pulled the MG under the drooping branches of a live oak. Got out and continued on foot, keeping close to the high stone wall.

The driveway was blocked by iron gates, set into massive pillars; the gates were locked, and an intercom system next to them was the only means of getting inside—an option not open to me. Through the bars I could see the blacktop stretching along an avenue of eucalyptus to a house on top of a rise: wood and stone, massive like the pillars. An old house, dating from the 1800s.

I stepped back and studied the wall. Too high to climb

easily and, besides, the wire strung along its top would be sure to trigger an alarm system. DeCarlo was a cautious man, intent on protecting what was his—including his "boy."

I went back to my car and settled down to wait. Maybe my visit would provoke some activity.

The sun was dipping behind the coastal ridge and the shadows were lengthening. I'd been sitting here for close to an hour, during which no one had arrived at or left the ranch. I was thirsty and uncomfortable, both from sitting in the cramped car and from the speculations that crowded my mind. My stomach growled; I lusted after a bacon cheeseburger.

In Monterey I'd spotted a Jack-in-the-Box, so I gave up the wait and headed back there.

7:51 P.M.

The offices of DeCarlo Enterprises in downtown Monterey were closed. I kept going through the business section and the tunnel under the Presidio to Lighthouse Avenue, then uphill to Archer Street. The windows of Austin DeCarlo's house glowed softly; a Jaguar and a BMW sat in its driveway. He was home, and he had company.

I was trying to decide whether it would be wise to approach him under such circumstances when the front door opened and two couples came out, went to the cars, and drove away. Seconds later the garage door slid up and a silver Lexus backed out; as the door slid down, I started my engine and prepared to follow.

To the cross street, right on Lighthouse, through the tunnel, and a series of jogs to Franklin Street. When the Lexus cut to the curb, I idled at a stop sign, watching the driver get out: a big man whose gray hair gleamed under the street-light as Joseph DeCarlo's had gleamed in the late-afternoon sunlight. His son? Had to be.

Austin DeCarlo went around and opened the other door for his passenger, a thin woman with a long cascade of dark hair, dressed in a flowing tunic-and-pants suit. As they walked hand in hand along the sidewalk, I parked and went after them.

Half a block ahead, a dozen or so people stood outside a restaurant, drinking wine and talking as they waited for tables. The smells borne on the breeze brought to mind my favorite Greek eatery in San Francisco. This one was called Epsilon, obviously a popular place. DeCarlo and the woman moved through the crowd and went inside. As I came closer I saw them being seated at a window table with the other couples who had earlier come out of his house.

I watched them through the window, feeling like a waif out of some silent-film melodrama. Ever since I'd studied that *Newsweek* photograph, I'd suspected that Austin De-Carlo and Saskia Hunter were my birth parents, and his father's reaction to me had more or less confirmed it. Approaching this man could change my life in ways I might not like. Perhaps knowing as much as I did was enough; I didn't need to have actual contact with him. Besides, this was a public place; he wouldn't appreciate me making a scene.

What do you care if he doesn't appreciate it? The man abandoned you before your birth. Hanging back on grounds of good manners is an excuse because you're afraid.

I pushed through the crowd and opened the restaurant's

door, waved the maitre d' aside and went over to the window table.

"Austin DeCarlo?" I said to the gray-haired man.

He'd been studying the wine list, and when he glanced up his mouth twitched in irritation. He had his father's strong features, but their lines were blunted by years of good living; the glaring eyes that turned up at me were the same faded blue. "Yes?" he snapped.

"My name's Sharon McCone. I believe you knew my great-aunt, Fenella."

His mouth sagged open and he stared at me. I stared back, at a loss for further words. After a moment he set down the wine list and ran an unsteady hand over his chin. Shook his head as if to deny what he was thinking. I remained speechless, afraid of what I'd set in motion.

The couples at the table leaned anxiously toward DeCarlo. The woman he was with touched his arm and asked, "Austin, darling, what's the matter?"

Her voice brought him back to his surroundings. He glanced almost furtively at the other diners, then back at me. "My God," he whispered, "you're the image of your mother!"

Even though I'd more or less expected such a reaction, DeCarlo's words caused a physical shock wave. Something caught in my chest and for a moment I felt as if my heart had stopped; then it began racing. I flashed hot and cold, and everything shifted—his face, the diners at his table, the rough-plastered walls, the tiled floor. I grasped the back of his chair for support.

He stood quickly, and through the riot of my emotions I heard him making excuses to his party—something about me being the daughter of an old friend, which sounded insincere to me and must have seemed the outright lie it was to them. I felt his hands grasp my shoulders none too gently as he began steering me toward the door. Saw diners at the other tables watching us with curiosity and concern. He didn't stop till we were several storefronts away, then turned me around and peered intently at my face. Shook his head—again trying to deny who I was.

I found my voice at last. "Let's go someplace where we can talk privately."

"I can't deny it," Austin DeCarlo said. "The proof's in your face."

We were seated at opposite ends of the sofa in a room that took up the entire third story of his house. The semi-circular windows on the north and south walls reflected us, father and daughter, our postures wary and tentative. In contrast, his Irish setter, Rupert, lay relaxed on the cushion between us.

At first DeCarlo had been downright skeptical of my story, demanding proof that I was who I claimed. I showed him my identification, the petition for adoption, and the *Newsweek* photograph, and then he began to internalize the fact that he was face to face with his forty-year-old daughter. Then, looking even more shaken, he went to light a fire and pour brandy.

Now I asked, "My mother—she was Saskia Hunter?"

"Yes."

"Is she still living?"

"Yes."

"Where?"

"Boise, Idaho."

"You're in touch with her?"

". . . Not really. It's complicated."

"How?" I raised the brandy snifter to my lips, my hand unsteady. In spite of the fire, I couldn't get warm.

"Let me start at the beginning." DeCarlo shifted toward me, hooking one elbow over the back of the sofa. "In 1958 I was traveling around the country with a friend. We were both sick and tired of the Valley, and my father and I hadn't been getting along. He wanted me to learn the family business so he could retire and ranch, but I couldn't see myself traveling from office to office to check up on how the plant-tissue analyses were going. So my friend and I bought a used Triumph and went on the road." He smiled. "I'd like to think we were forerunners of the guys on *Route Sixty-six*, but I suppose in reality we were pretty naive and small-town."

I jiggled my foot, both nervous and impatient. The last thing I needed now was a fond reminiscence about his youthful travels.

He noticed my impatience and hurried on with his story. "Anyway, after five months the car broke down in Fort Hall, Idaho, and while we were stuck there waiting for parts, I met your mother. She was seventeen—pretty, smart, and had a wild streak. Her parents didn't want her to see me, but she'd sneak off and meet me at the auto court where my friend and I were staying. When the car was fixed, he bought out my interest and moved on. I rented a room from some friends of Kia's and took a job in a café. Before long she moved in with me, and in the winter she got pregnant."

"So you left her."

He narrowed his eyes, stung by the accusatory note in my voice. "That's not the way it was."

"How, then?"

He made a tentative move to touch my shoulder, stopped

midway. "Look, I know this isn't easy for you. It certainly isn't for me. Can we not make judgments just yet?"

"You mean, can *I* not make judgments. I'll try. Did you love her, Austin?" I didn't know why whether I'd been conceived in love or not should matter, but it did.

He considered for a moment. "I thought I loved Kia. I must have, because I asked her to marry me, even though we hadn't been getting along for some time. And she must've loved me, because she accepted. But she was still underage, and her parents wouldn't consent, so we decided to run off to Nevada. Then the photograph of us with Fenella McCone appeared in *Newsweek*."

"Fenella was a relative of Saskia's."

"Distant, but she was very fond of her. I've always suspected she had a hand in your adoption. Kia hadn't known her long, but she told me she knew she could always turn to her in an emergency. And I guess she did."

"So the photograph appeared in *Newsweek* . . ."

"And my father saw it. Up till then, he had no idea I was living with Kia. I went home before Christmas, stayed a couple of weeks—which didn't please Kia one bit—and gave him a story about working on a ranch outside of Billings, Montana. He approved of that, assumed that eventually I'd come home for good."

"What did he do when he found out where you really were?"

"Chartered a plane and flew to Idaho, intent on dragging me home. He's a difficult man—"

The scene at his ranch flashed through my mind. "Difficult? He's a control freak!"

DeCarlo raised his eyebrows. "You *know* him?"

"I spoke with him briefly this afternoon, right before he set his security guy on me."

"Tony? Did he hurt you?"

"No. I can take care of myself."

He smiled faintly. "You sound like Kia. She's one tough woman. Of course, I'm pretty tough myself. You inherited a double dose—"

"No," I said, bristling at his laying claim to how I'd turned out, "I get that from my adoptive parents."

DeCarlo was silent for a moment. "Did you tell my father who you are?"

"Didn't have to. He figured it out right away. Said the same thing you did—that I look like Saskia Hunter. Anyway, he arrived on the reservation . . ."

"And a friend warned us in time. He loaned us his truck, and we decided to skip Nevada and go to northern California, where Kia's favorite uncle lived. She thought he'd let us stay with him, maybe lend us some money. And he agreed to, but my father traced us, busted into his house a few days later. Kia wasn't there, she'd gone to the store for some groceries. My father sent me home with his ranch foreman, said he'd take care of things. And . . . I went. I never even got to tell her good-bye."

I frowned. "Weren't you kind of old to be following your father's orders?"

He leaned forward, propping his elbows on his knees, head drooping. "Yeah, I was, but where my father's concerned I've never been a strong man. Back then, in many ways, I was just a boy."

Just a boy, in his twenties. I couldn't relate to that. By the time I was the age he'd been when he left Saskia Hunter, I was working to pay my college tuition bills.

"So you just left Saskia to your father's mercies," I said.

"Her Uncle Ray was there to protect her."

"She had to rely on an uncle, rather than the man who'd made her pregnant."

DeCarlo closed his eyes. "Sharon, I thought you weren't going to make judgments."

"It's damned hard not to. As a woman, I can empathize only too well with her predicament." I took a deep breath, got my anger under control. "Okay, what happened when your father came back to the ranch?"

"He said he'd taken care of things by settling money on Kia, and that she'd told him she never wanted to see me again."

"You *believed* that?"

He hunched his shoulders, rolled his empty snifter between his palms. "As I said before, Kia and I hadn't been getting along. And I had no reason to doubt my father; he'd thrown money at problems my whole life."

Problems: two human lives, my mother's and mine. That's all we'd been to him.

"You never tried to find her?" I asked. "Or me?" My voice was raw with hurt.

He didn't notice; he was caught up in his own pain. "I found her a year later. She was living in Moscow, Idaho, planning to start college there in the fall. She told me she'd put you up for adoption. She was afraid if she kept you, my father might try to take you away from her."

I pictured the expression on the old man's face as he'd loomed over me that afternoon. "Not too damn likely! He didn't want any half-breed granddaughter perching on his family tree. Hanging from it, maybe."

". . . He's not that bad."

"I'll have to take your word for it. So that was the end? You just decided to pretend I didn't exist?"

"I didn't want to, but Kia was very angry with me and refused to tell me anything about the adoption."

I drained my snifter, held it out for a refill—giving myself time to cool down. Maybe he was right; maybe I was too quick to judge. After all, he'd been frank with me, admitting to his errors and weakness. When he passed the glass back, I asked, "Do you know what happened to my mother after that?"

"She completed college and law school at the University of Idaho. Married a fellow attorney, Thomas Blackhawk. They were in private practice together in Boise, and since he died a few years ago she's devoted her efforts to Indian causes."

Saskia Blackhawk. The name was vaguely familiar. Maybe I'd read about her somewhere.

"Did she have other children?"

"A son and a daughter. They're in their twenties now."

I felt an odd twinge. My birth mother had given me up, but gone on to have other children. I had a half brother and sister who probably weren't aware I existed. "You know a good bit about her," I said. "Why did you follow her life and career?"

". . . I thought you might initiate a search and get in touch with her."

"You could've initiated a search yourself. There're plenty of resources."

"I know." He shook his head wearily. "But by the time they became available, so many years had gone by . . ."

So many years, and here I sat with a stranger. A man who described himself as tough, but in reality was weak. A weak man who was my father, but didn't seem like a father. Suddenly my anger drained and all I felt was empty. I needed to be alone.

When I said I had to go, DeCarlo protested. He wanted to hear about my life. He wanted me to be his houseguest. I refused, told him I'd call in the morning. Then I fled to the refuge of an impersonal room on motel row.

LISTENING . . .

"Is she still living?"
"Yes."
"Where?"
"Boise, Idaho."
"You're in touch with her?"
". . . Not really. It's complicated."

That's a significant silence. You're either in touch or not in touch with someone. What's complicated about that?

"Not really" implies a degree. Is he saying he's been in touch with Saskia Hunter Blackhawk since she told him she put me up for adoption? Recently, perhaps?

About what? Me? Somehow I doubt that.

"Why did you follow her life and career?"
". . . I thought you might initiate a search and get in touch with her."

"*You could've initiated a search yourself. There're plenty of resources.*"

"*I know. But by the time they became available, so many years had gone by . . .*"

Listen to that hesitation. He's not being candid about his interest in Saskia. It isn't because of me; in the next breath he all but admits he'd given up on locating me. The way his words trail off tells me he didn't really care that much anymore.

So why keep track of Saskia? Does he still love her? No, he's not sure he ever did. They're connected for some other reason now. And it *is* complicated.

Tuesday

·

SEPTEMBER 12

12:31 A.M.

"Shar, are you *ever* gonna let me get a decent night's sleep?"

"Just one favor, Mick. One little favor. Did you locate any material on DeCarlo Enterprises' Spirit Lake development?"

"Yeah. It's on your desk at the office."

"Oh."

"What's wrong?"

"I need you to fax it to me at my motel in Monterey. Right away."

Sigh. "Okay, I can do that pretty quick. What's the fax number there?"

I read it to him.

"I suppose you dragged the motel clerk out of bed to get use of their machine?"

"Not exactly. He was dozing in front of the TV."

"Someday I'm gonna have T-shirts printed up. They'll say 'I was robbed of my sleep by Sharon McCone.' I'll sell millions, make my fortune."

*   *   *

I read the curl of flimsy paper with growing shock as I sat on the bed in my motel room. My natural father had shaded the truth when it came to his current connection with my birth mother.

Shaded? Hell, he'd painted it pink and tied it up in pretty ribbons!

The information Mick had provided said that DeCarlo's Spirit Lake project was embroiled in controversy. A group of Modoc Indians in the nearby town of Sage Rock had brought suit against the development company, claiming tribal ownership of the lake and a thousand surrounding acres, stemming from an 1860 treaty with the federal government. The Modocs considered the lake sacred, and were opposed to any form of development.

In a brief filed with the U.S. District Court, an attorney for DeCarlo Enterprises stated that the 1860 treaty was unauthorized by the government. Furthermore, the only valid treaty between the tribe and the federal authorities was negotiated in 1864, and removed the Modocs from California to a Klamath Indian reserve in Oregon.

The Indian advocate who would be arguing the case countered that the 1860 treaty had been negotiated in good faith on the part of the Modocs; the tribe should not be penalized because they believed in the federal agent's authority to do so. Various precedents were cited, and the brief petitioned for the return of Spirit Lake and the surrounding acreage to the Modocs.

The Indian advocate was Saskia Blackhawk.

No wonder DeCarlo had hesitated when I asked if he was currently in touch with her. No wonder he'd concealed the reason he'd kept track of her. My natural father seemed as capable of deceit as my adoptive parents.

What to do? The logical course of action would be to

confront Austin DeCarlo with my knowledge. Or talk with Saskia Blackhawk. Clarify the situation.

But the logical course of action doesn't always fit with the dictates of one's emotions. Instead, I got up, threw the few things I'd unpacked back into my travel bag, and drove straight for Hy's ranch in Mono County.

8:27 A.M.

Hy was asleep when I looked into the master bedroom of the ranchhouse, but at my first step he came fully awake and primed for action, as he always did when startled—a consequence of too much dangerous living in a long-ago incarnation. When he saw me, he relaxed, grinned, and swept away the covers.

"Nice surprise, McCone. Take off your clothes and hop on in here."

Although the sight of his long, lean body enticed me, I shook my head. "Not now. I need to talk with you."

"If you're turning me down, it must be serious. Give me a minute. Coffeemaker's loaded; all you have to do is start it."

I went to the kitchen, flipped the switch on the machine, and sat at the table. The room was pretty much as I imagined it had been when he was growing up here: black-and-white linoleum, white enameled cabinets with scalloped underpanels, yellow Formica countertops, vintage range and fridge. The table matched the counters, the chairs were tubular chrome with red plastic seats. Retro all the way, and a collectibles dealer would probably kill for the contents of the drawers and cupboards. I was glad Hy had left the house virtually unchanged, because it conveyed a sense of permanence and continuity. The world might be veering out of control, but this was a refuge that connected us to a saner past.

The coffeemaker started puffing steam. As I fetched cups, Hy came into the room wearing his bathrobe, hair wet and curly from a quick shower. He brought the carafe to me and poured, kissed me on the forehead. "Okay," he said, "what's this talk that can't wait?"

"I found my birth father."

He paused in the process of setting the carafe on the warmer, then came over and sat down. "Tell me about him."

As I recounted what had happened since we'd last spoken, I watched his reactions. Long ago we'd discovered we were each other's touchstones—a metallurgist's term after which we'd named our coast property. A touchstone is a black siliceous rock used to test the purity of silver or gold; similarly, we used each other to test the validity of our responses to people and situations. Neither of us had ever failed the other, and I could tell from his expression that he was now validating my reactions to Austin and the current problem—save one.

"You can't run away," he told me.

"I know, but I'm on such overload."

"You're on overload because you still don't know everything. You need to get the whole story."

"You mean talk with my . . . mother."

He nodded.

"And then?"

"Take it where it leads you."

6:37 P.M.

Hy had suggested I fly the Cessna from Tufa Lake to Boise; he had a meeting in San Francisco the next day, and could drive down in my car. I agreed to taking the plane, but I wanted to put in some time at the office and pick up clean clothes, so after catching a few hours' sleep, I flew to Oakland and drove into the city in the old car Hy kept garaged near North Field.

When I got to Pier 24½, Ted was still at his desk, looking very much the capable administrator in spite of his wild Hawaiian shirt—a new fashion statement for a man who, as long as I'd known him, had favored elegant vests or jackets with his jeans. Today he seemed tired, but it was a good weariness, reflecting a day of challenges well met; he thrived on being in charge.

"Maybe it's time I promoted you," I said from the door of his office.

He started and looked up. "Shar, you're back! Promoted me to what?"

I went inside, removed a stack of books from a bar stool that had inexplicably appeared there a few weeks ago, and sat down. This was as good a time as any to discuss some upcoming changes at the pier.

"I don't have a title in mind," I said. "Grand Pooh-Bah? How does that sound?"

"I like it. But what does a Grand Pooh-Bah do?"

"Runs the place when I'm not around. I'm getting stale; I need to be out in the field more."

"Fine by me, but won't that be stepping on Rae's toes? You've always put her in charge."

"She's quitting to work on her novel."

"Ah, the infamous manuscript that she won't even discuss with Ricky. Well, I wish her luck. But what about my work for Altman and Zahn? D'you think I can handle both jobs?" Ted also managed Anne-Marie and Hank's law office next door.

"That's something I've been meaning to discuss with you: they're expanding and need more space, so they're looking to move across the Embarcadero to Hills Plaza."

Ted's face went still, as it always did when he was absorbing unwelcome news.

I added, "They haven't told anybody but me, because the lease hasn't been negotiated yet. But even if that deal falls through, it's only a matter of time."

"And they didn't express any interest in taking me along," he said flatly.

"On the contrary, we fought over you and I won."

"Don't I have any say in the matter?"

"Of course you do, but I already knew what you'd decide. In spite of their being good friends and your work history in the legal area, I'm aware you're not crazy about the law."

". . . True. But I'll miss them." Briefly he looked pensive, then asked, "So how'd you lay claim to me?"

"Let's just say that you may be the only Grand Pooh-Bah in the city who was won in a poker game."

"Good Lord. Well, I accept your offer, title and all."

"Comes with a raise, too. And I plan to hire you an assistant, as well as take on a couple of new operatives."

"Where'll we put them? Our space is full."

"We're taking over Altman and Zahn's suite."

"Business is that good? Well, of course it is. I should know; I'm the one who sends out the invoices." He frowned.

"What's wrong?"

"Oh, I was just flashing on the old days. You lived in that

dreadful studio on Guerrero and the rest of us were crammed into the Victorian in Bernal Heights. Most people would've called it a wretched existence, but all we cared about was saving the world."

"Well, one small legal cooperative wasn't going to accomplish that. Besides, what's wrong with being able to pay our bills and live like grownups?"

"Nothing, but in some weird way I think that you and I are still out to save the world."

"Not the world, but some of its people anyway. We thought too big back then. Thinking small is more realistic."

"Yeah, but right now I'm more interested in thinking big. Just how much of a raise are we talking about?"

Ted had left a stack of message slips in my office, all of them from clients, except one from Austin DeCarlo, asking that I call him. I lined it up with the edge of my desk and tapped my fingers against it as I considered what to do. Finally I picked up the phone and dialed. DeCarlo answered immediately.

"What happened to you?" he asked. "You said you'd call in the morning. I'd hoped to spend the day getting to know you."

". . . Something came up with an important client, and I had to get back here. I was going to call you later." An outright lie. He and I had certainly gotten off on a fine footing!

"I could fly up there tomorrow."

"I'm sorry, I'm going out of town."

"Oh, where?"

I couldn't pile one falsehood upon another. "Boise. I need to see my . . . mother."

Silence. "Well, I'm sure you do. But I'd like to see you first."

Of course he would; he wanted to explain about the Spirit Lake project in a way that wouldn't turn me against him. "Austin . . . It *is* okay if I call you that? At this late date I can't see me calling you Daddy."

He laughed. "I can't imagine being called Daddy. Austin's fine. What were you about to say?"

"I know about Spirit Lake and the lawsuit."

More silence.

"I also suspect that you and Saskia are still angry at each other, even after all these years, and being on opposite sides of this suit hasn't helped any. So I'm keeping an open mind, and I'll continue to do so no matter what she tells me."

"You're a wise woman."

"Hardly. But I've seen enough misery in my work to know what kinds of traps people's emotions can set. I don't intend to get snared by any—Saskia's or yours."

"Well, have a safe trip, then. I suppose it's not politic to send my regards to your mother, but extend them if you think otherwise. And call me when you get back; I'll fly up and spend some time with you."

As I replaced the receiver I reflected that only the experience of growing up in the dysfunctional McCone household could have prepared me for navigating the emotional potholes and pitfalls of this new familial territory.

Wednesday

·

SEPTEMBER 13

2:40 P.M.

Boise looked pretty from the air. It was surrounded by desert, where irrigation channels cut furrows in the land and cultivated fields stood out in checkerboard relief against the brown. A river, flanked by greenbelt, snaked along the edge of the city center; tall buildings and the dome of the state capitol gleamed in the afternoon sun. Beyond them, housing tracts had begun their insidious creep toward the mountains to the north and east.

I'd learned from an article in the airline magazine that Boise, and Idaho as a whole, were among the fastest-growing areas in the country. State and federal government and a broad-based economy provided jobs of all sorts, and a low cost of living had lured skilled people from many other areas, including my own. The man seated next to me—the talkative type I generally try to avoid, but whose chatter I welcomed on this emotionally tense flight—commuted twice a week between his home in Santa Clara and his job at Micron Technology's Boise offices, and he hoped to move his family to Idaho as soon as their Silicon Valley house sold.

Even the airport strengthened Boise's appeal: although I had only a carry-on bag, as I walked by the carousel I noticed that the luggage from my flight was already coming up. There were no long lines at the rental-car counters, and the vehicles, for most companies at least, were only steps away. A friendly clerk highlighted on the map an uncomplicated route to Eighth Street in the north end of town, where Blackhawk & Blackhawk was located.

The law firm occupied an older house in a block of tree-shaded residences, many of which had been converted to commercial use. It was a frame, two stories, with a deep, pillared front porch and a steeply peaked roof above a round attic window. Satiny red-and-green trim stood out against light gray paint, and the lawn and hedges were well barbered; obviously my birth mother liked things well maintained, and her law practice was profitable.

I parked the car in the shade of an old Dutch elm whose leaves were beginning to turn and sat there for a while. The afternoon was warmish, the street quiet, but I felt chilled and my thoughts were anything but tranquil. A gray squirrel scampered across the pavement, and I watched it with rapt concentration. I was experiencing the same ambivalence as I had outside the restaurant in Monterey, before I confronted Austin DeCarlo. But this time the emotion was stronger and more complex, as feelings often are in a woman's relationship to her mother; DeCarlo had hardly been a player in the drama surrounding my birth, but Saskia Hunter had been its leading lady.

On Monday night I could have turned and walked away without ever coming face to face with DeCarlo. I wasn't in that deep, and merely knowing who my birth parents were might have been enough. But instead I'd taken that irrevocable step, and now that I'd heard his story, I needed to hear Saskia's as well. So I began playing a mental game of devil's advocate to make myself get out of the car.

You don't have to do this. You can drive away and never look back.

But I'd regret it my whole life.

The woman gave you up at birth. She's probably a lousy person. And friends and clients notwithstanding, you're not wild about lawyers.

She gave me up so I wouldn't fall into Joseph DeCarlo's clutches. And she isn't a typical lawyer; she works for the good of her people.

She won't be happy to see you, though. She has two children of her own. She's probably known where you were your whole life and didn't care.

Maybe she had those children partly to make up for what she lost. Maybe Fenella didn't tell her who adopted me.

Do you really believe that?

I want to, and I'm going in there.

Handwoven rugs in brilliant colors lay against the hardwood floor of the house's entry. A steep staircase with a mahogany handrail rose to the second story. An arrow on a sign that said RECEPTION pointed to the right. I stepped through an archway, saw a young woman whose black hair was caught up in a ponytail and tied with a red scarf staring at a computer monitor. A woman who, in profile, looked very much as I had in my twenties. A plaque on the desk said ROBIN BLACKHAWK.

My half sister. I wanted to back out of the room and run like hell.

"Be with you in a minute," she said without looking away from the screen. "This is a new machine, and I think it's possessed by demons." She moved the mouse, clicked, and exclaimed, "Dammit! D'you know anything about iMacs?"

"I have one myself. What's the problem?"

"A friend loaned me this software, and apparently he didn't register the game with the manufacturer. A warning popped up and now I can't get it off there."

I stepped around the desk so I could see the monitor. A poker game was displayed against a dark-green background, a window with a notice superimposed on it.

"What am I gonna do?" Robin Blackhawk muttered. "When I click on the window and try to go to something else, it just pops up again. My mother'll kill me for playing on the job."

"Just turn off the machine. And when you restart, don't call up the game again."

"You're a genius!"

"Hardly. But I've had the same problem myself, when I didn't realize some software I borrowed from my nephew wasn't registered."

She shut the machine off, then swiveled toward me, and I got my first straight-on view of her face. Her lips were fuller, her nose more prominent, her forehead higher, but we resembled each other strongly. She saw it too, and her eyes widened.

"Do I know you?" she asked.

"No, but we're related." I gave her one of my cards. When she glanced at it, I saw the name meant nothing to her. "I'd like to see your mother."

"Mom's in court all day, but I can make an appointment for you. How about eight o'clock this evening?"

"Eight's fine. Does she usually take evening appointments?"

"Evening, midnight, six in the morning—you name it. Mom's a workaholic, and it doesn't help that we live upstairs." She eyed me curiously. "You're related on her side of the family, right?"

"Yes."

"I've never met any of the Hunters."

"How come?"

"She hasn't been on speaking terms with them since her teens. I don't know why. She doesn't like to talk about it. What's your connection to us?"

"It's kind of complicated. Maybe I'll understand it better after I talk with her."

8:03 P.M.

Lights glowed both upstairs and down in the Blackhawk house when I returned that evening. I didn't have to talk myself out of the car this time, but my tension level went over the top as I approached. When I stepped inside I saw Robin, still seated at her desk.

"You getting along any better with that thing?" I asked, motioning at the iMac.

"Yeah. It's an easy machine." She shut it off and got up. "Mom's not home yet. She had a dinner meeting with a client, and I expected her by now, but I guess it ran over. Would you like to wait in the parlor?"

"Sure. Thanks." I followed her across the hall to a high-ceilinged room furnished with plain sofas and chairs upholstered in beige and brown. The walls were bare, except for an irregularly shaped piece of hide painted with buffalo, horses, and warriors that hung over the redbrick fireplace.

Robin saw me looking at it. "It's elk hide, the only thing of her family's that Mom has. Her favorite uncle gave it to her when she was a child."

"Your father," I said, sitting down on a sofa. "Was he Shoshone?"

"No, Sioux." She sat down across from me, looked intently at my face. "You really resemble Mom and me. Darcy, too, except for the purple hair."

"Darcy?"

"My younger brother. All through high school and college he's the all-American kid. Then he hooks up with this weird crowd, and all of a sudden he's got purple hair, a nose stud, earrings, and a nipple ring. Probably some other hardware that he hadn't treated me to the sight of, thank God. If you ask me, twenty-four is too old to get into that kind of stuff."

Great. I had a bemetaled half brother with purple hair. And I thought Joey was strange. . . .

"Where does Darcy work?"

"KIVI, local TV station. Channel Six. Behind the scenes, of course. He's a video editor. Boise just isn't ready for somebody with purple hair coanchoring the evening news."

"And you work for your mother?"

"For now. I'm starting law school next spring. For years I resisted following in Mom's and Dad's footsteps, but I found out by working here that the law fascinates me."

"You're how many years older than Darcy?"

"Two years chronologically, two decades emotionally."

So Saskia Blackhawk had waited fourteen years after my birth to have another child. Of course, at least seven of those would have been devoted to her education, the remainder to establishing the law practice.

Robin glanced at her watch. "I can't imagine what's keeping Mom. She budgets her time strictly. If she says she'll be someplace, she's there to the minute."

"Did she check in with you after I made the appointment?" It occurred to me that if she heard my name, she might try to avoid seeing me.

"No, she—" The phone on the reception desk rang, and Robin went to answer it.

I got up and moved to the fireplace, studied the elk skin painting. The warriors were primitive, almost stick figures, but the buffalo and horses were fully and lovingly fleshed out. How on earth had I, who hated huge beasts, sprung from such a people?

Behind me I heard Robin gasp and then moan. The receiver clattered into its cradle. I turned, saw her coming across the hallway, pale and agitated.

"That was the emergency room at Saint Alphonsus," she said. "Mom's been hurt. Jesus, it sounds bad. I've got to go to her."

My stomach lurched. "What happened?"

"Hit-and-run." She began digging frantically through her purse. "Dammit, I can't find my car keys!"

"Don't worry about that," I said. "I'll drive you."

The media had already been alerted to the hit-and-run of a prominent activist attorney; press vans clogged the parking area in front of the emergency entrance of St. Alphonsus Hospital, and reporters with microphones and minicams waited on the sidewalk. I had to push them back as I guided Robin to the doors. Once inside, she was taken away by two detectives from the Boise P.D.'s Crimes Against

Persons unit, who wanted to talk with her about her mother's accident.

The presence of the detectives unnerved me. In most jurisdictions, such accidents were handled by uniformed officers from a traffic-safety detail; plainclothes officers indicated that this might be more than a simple hit-and-run. As I sat in the waiting room, I could do nothing more than agonize and speculate.

Emergency wards are awful places at any time, but particularly at night—full of glaring fluorescence, harried personnel, distraught and often bloodied people. St. Alphonsus's was no exception. A long line snaked across the floor to the admitting desk. Friends and relatives of the seriously injured sat in stunned and anxious silence, while the less seriously injured suffered. Somewhere nearby a man kept uttering long, demented wails.

Normally I had difficulty dealing with such situations, but this was unbearable. Somewhere in the hospital my birth mother lay injured, possibly dying, and I was powerless to go to her, unable to learn the details of her condition. If only I'd told Robin I was her half sister, I might have been allowed in on the conversation with the officers. But to her I was nothing more than a distant relative, and to them, if they'd noticed me at all, simply someone who had volunteered to drive her here. Already Saskia Blackhawk could have died without either of us setting eyes upon the other—

"Sharon." Robin's voice. I stood up, saw she'd been crying.

"How is she?"

"In surgery, that's all I know. The rest . . . it's bad. The police say the hit-and-run wasn't an accident. Somebody lured her away from the restaurant and deliberately ran her over."

I took her arm, pulled her aside as an orderly pushed a gurney past us. "Let's sit down and you can tell me about it."

The police theory was well founded. Saskia had been having dinner with a representative of the Coeur d'Alene tribe, who were suing the government over fishing rights on their native lands, at Milford's Fish House in the Eighth Street Marketplace downtown. Her pager went off around seven forty-five, and she excused herself to find a pay phone and return the call. She didn't come back to the table.

According to another patron, Saskia spoke on the phone for less than two minutes, then left the restaurant. An employee who had been taking his break out front told the detectives she had turned toward the river on Eighth Street, rather than toward the garage where Milford's validated parking for diners. When the police checked, they found her 1999 Ford Escort still parked there.

Approximately fifteen minutes after she left Milford's, Saskia was struck by a blue Datsun traveling at high speed along Tenth Street between Miller and River Streets—an industrial area, mostly deserted at night. A witness who was returning home to a nearby housing project called in the accident to 911. He told the responding officers that the car had been idling a block away when Saskia turned the corner onto Tenth; its driver gunned the engine, shot across the intersection, swerved to hit her, and sped away—but not before the witness got its license-plate number. Half an hour later the Datsun, which had been reported stolen late that afternoon, was found abandoned and wiped clean of prints several blocks away.

"Sounds like a professional job," I said to Robin.

"That's what the police think."

"Those pagers—don't they show the number of the last person who called?"

"It was smashed when Mom was hit. The police accessed the number she called from the restaurant—a cell phone whose ownership is proving difficult to trace."

"Probably one of those illegal cloned ones."

Robin nodded, running both hands over her face. "Sharon, they were asking about Mom's enemies, and they want to come by in the morning to go over the files of her active cases. I said I couldn't let them do that—confidentiality—but I agreed to summarize them."

"It could help. Defending the causes she does, your mother must've made enemies."

"Well, sure. But I can't imagine . . . The client she was having dinner with? That has to do with the Coeur d'Alene's rights to fish lands that the feds're leasing to a lumber company. The cause isn't popular with the company and loggers in general, but you don't run a person down for defending it. And there's another case in California—most of her work is on the federal level—that she told me was turning personal. She's going up against this developer that she's got bad history with. But she didn't seem afraid he'd *kill* her."

Austin DeCarlo. Once the police started investigating, the story of that bad history would be dragged to light, and the press would get wind of it. Then neither he nor I nor any member of the Blackhawk or McCone families would be able to prevent it from becoming public.

I asked, "Did she say what this bad history was?"

"No. Mom's a private person; I was surprised she told me anything at all. Normally she wouldn't've, except he or his attorney did something to set her off."

"When was this?"

"Last month. I don't remember the exact—"

"Ms. Blackhawk?" A woman spoke behind us.

We both stood, turned to the doctor. She looked grim and tired; her attempt at a reassuring smile was a grotesque caricature.

"My mother," Robin asked. "Is she going to be okay?"

"Why don't we go someplace where we can talk quietly?"

The news was not encouraging. Saskia Blackhawk had suffered broken bones, extensive internal injuries, trauma to the head, and was in a coma. The surgeon had repaired the most serious injuries, and Saskia had been placed on the critical list and taken to intensive care.

Robin asked to see her mother. At first Dr. Bishop refused, but seeing her distress, she relented and allowed her a brief visit. Once again I, the outsider, was left to indulge my private fears.

The emergency-room business had picked up—a major crash on Interstate 84, someone said. Ambulances sped in and out of the drive, dropping off personnel and people on gurneys at the side entrance. Other people rushed in through the front, desperate for news of friends and loved ones. When I could take the pain and commotion no longer, I went to the deserted vending room and called Hy, who was staying at my house.

"Jesus, McCone," he said after I'd filled him in, "do they think she'll pull through?"

"They're not saying either way."

"Be a shame if you never got to talk with her. You gonna tell Robin you're her sister?"

"I'll have to, pretty soon. She's already asked how we're related, and when I tell her I'm staying around for a while, she'll really start to wonder."

"So you'll be there how long?"

"Till the situation's resolved one way or the other. I want to keep tabs on the police investigation; there may be something I can do to help. Besides, I want to see Saskia, even if—"

"I know, McCone. And I'll be thinking of you."

"Thanks. I— Oh, Robin just walked by looking for me. Got to go. Love you."

"Love you too. Take care."

Robin was crying softly when we got into my rental car. With far more conviction than I felt, I said, "It'll be all right."

"She's so . . . It was like she was dead. And those beeping machines and the tubes . . . I *hate* this!"

"I know."

"And now I've gotta call Darcy, and what am I gonna tell him that won't send him over the edge?"

"Over the edge?"

She nodded, digging a tissue from her purse. "Darce is . . . He's not exactly unstable. It's just that when things don't go right, he gets agitated in a major way."

Meaning Darcy *was* unstable. "You said he works for Channel Six?"

"Right."

"Then you'd better call him right away. They had a reporter at the hospital."

"Oh, shit! For sure he already knows!"

I reached into my bag for my phone, handed it to her. She punched in the number, waited, ended the call. "No answer. God, I hope he hasn't—"

"Hasn't what?"

"I don't know. I never know what he'll do. Darce is my

brother and I love him, but he's . . . Oh, hell, he's really a mess."

Welcome to another dysfunctional family, McCone.

I said, "Okay, I'll help you find him. We'll deal with the problem."

We'd reached her house, and I pulled to the curb and shut the engine off. Robin undid her seat belt and leaned toward me, eyes focused on my face. "Why're you doing this for me?"

"I like you and I want to help."

"And we're family, but you won't tell me how."

"It's not that I won't—"

"Yes, it is. You're avoiding the subject."

"Look, you've had a difficult evening—"

"You know," she said, still watching me closely, "a few years ago I was poking around in a box of Mom's old papers, looking for a picture I'd drawn for her in third grade that I wanted to show my boyfriend. And I came across a letter to her from somebody called Fenella. It was dated 1963, and it said—I memorized most of it—it said, 'Your little girl is doing fine. She's healthy, bright, and happy with her family. You made a loving decision, the best you could under the circumstances.'

"When I showed the letter to Mom, she blew up, told me never to go through her things. I begged her to tell me why she gave the baby up and where she was. She said the subject was closed, and her tone scared me so much I never dared to try to find out anything on my own." She paused, took a deep breath. "That baby was you, wasn't she, Sharon?"

". . . Yes." In a way, it was a relief to have it out in the open.

Robin looked down at her hands and started to cry again.

Oh, God, I thought. She doesn't need this, not now, and she'll hate me for it!

I said, "I'm sorry this comes at such a bad time."

She mumbled something.

"What?"

"I said there's nothing to be sorry about. You don't know how often I've dreamed of finding you. And then, on the absolute worst day of my life, you showed up and helped me get through it."

As Robin and I climbed the porch steps, a figure moved in the shadows—a wiry figure of about my height, whose head looked misshapen. I braced myself for trouble, but she sighed in relief. "Darce! So this is where you've been."

"Robbie? I heard about Mom, but I couldn't stand to go to the hospital, so I came here." The little-boy inflection of his words didn't match the deep timbre of his voice.

Robin unlocked the door, reached inside to put on the overhead light, and I got my first look at my half brother. She'd told me about the purple hair, but hadn't mentioned that it poufed high and wide above his scalp, so he resembled a stick of cotton candy. His face was a more masculine version of hers and his upper lip was stubbled with an unsuccessful attempt at a mustache; silver studs glittered in both nostrils; a feathered earring hung from his right lobe; a pair of small silver circlets pierced one eyebrow. He wore black jeans and a black tee emblazoned in glowing silver: DEEMONZ!

"Robbie?" he said again. "Is Mom . . . ?"

"She's out of surgery." She went to him, took his arm. "Let's go inside and I'll tell you about it."

"I want to stay here. Can't you turn out that light?" He squinted up at it.

Robin took a closer look at him. "What're you on?"

"I just smoked some dope, is all."

"Uh-huh."

"Look, don't start on me, okay?"

"What good would it do?" She glanced apologetically at me, and Darcy noticed my presence.

"Who the hell's this?"

"A friend. She drove me to the hospital."

"She looks like Mom."

"She's also a relative."

"Mom's relative? She doesn't deal with those people."

". . . Well, this one she will. Come on inside, Darce."

He hung back, staring at me. "What's your name?"

"Sharon McCone." I offered my hand.

He ignored it. "How're you related to my mother? Where're you from?"

"Darcy!" Robin tugged hard on his arm. "Inside! We've got to talk about Mom." This time he offered no resistance, but kept staring at me over his shoulder as they went through the door.

I stayed on the porch, leaning against a pillar and breathing in the cold midnight air. Robin would want to reassure her brother, and she would do better if she didn't have to sugarcoat the truth in front of me.

Thursday

·

SEPTEMBER 14

3:09 A.M.

Sounds in the night.

They'd woken me up and I lay in the four-poster bed in the Blackhawk guest room, listening. A floorboard creaked again below, and something bumped faintly. Robin, unable to sleep? Darcy, stumbling around under the influence of the sleeping pill his sister had given him, after insisting he spend the night in his old room rather than return to his apartment?

Maybe, maybe not. I tried to convince myself I was imagining a strange presence in the house, but the sounds struck me as furtive.

I slipped from beneath the down comforter, put on my borrowed robe. Cold air drifted under the room's closed door, as if another door or window was open somewhere. I turned the knob, peered out into darkness. If Robin or Darcy were moving about, they'd have put on a light. Well, maybe Darcy wouldn't—

Another creak, closer. Where? Probably on the staircase.

I groped on the dresser for my purse, found my small

flashlight. When I looked through the door again, a faint glow had appeared in the stairwell. It moved upward, and a shadow spread over the wall: huge, distorted, moving slowly and stealthily.

Intruder. No question of it.

I put my finger on the switch of my flashlight, wishing I had my .357 Magnum instead. I'd let whoever it was come to the top of the stairs, then take him or her by surprise.

Something groaned at the far end of the hall. It sounded to me like the house settling, but the intruder stopped and the light went out. I waited, listening. Caught something that wasn't a sound exactly, but more like the rhythm of the person's breathing. Wondered if he'd identified mine. Seconds passed, and then I heard a soft footfall. On the move again.

Now I could see the faint outline of a head against the stairwell wall. The intruder was nearly to the top. I aimed my flash that way, flicked on the switch. Glimpsed a thick-fingered hand and gleaming black metal—

The bullet smacked into the door frame only inches from me, and the shot's boom set my eardrums throbbing as I dove back into the guest room. I flattened on the floor, trying to think what I could use as a weapon. Footsteps thundered down the stairs, scrambled in the lower hallway, slapped across the porch and down its steps.

I let out my breath in a long sigh, then shakily got to my feet. My ears were ringing. In the hall Robin was screaming my name. I ran out there, collided with her. "That was a shot!" she exclaimed. "What happened?"

I steadied her. "Somebody broke into the house, was coming upstairs. He's gone now."

"Oh, my God! He shot at *you*?"

"Yeah." I went over and trained my flashlight on the door frame till I located the point of impact. Four inches to the left, and the bullet would've penetrated my skull. My hands went clammy; my skin rippled.

Robin's eyes followed the beam. She shuddered. "Did you . . . did you see who it was?"

"A man, I think. That's all." I glanced down the hall toward Darcy's room. "How could he sleep through all this?"

"That sleeping pill . . . I doubled the dosage. He's out for the night and most of the morning."

"Is that a good thing to do?"

"His doctor okayed it for when he's really stressed."

I wanted to ask her what exactly was wrong with Darcy, but I had more immediate things to attend to. "Robin, have there been any burglaries in the neighborhood recently?"

"No. It's relatively crime-free."

"What about suspicious characters? People who might steal for drug money?"

"Not that I know of."

"Does Darcy have any friends who might want to break in here? Do you?"

"My friends're pretty much like me—working too hard to think of much else. Darce's . . . Well, I hate to say it, but they're either too stoned or too lazy."

"Any old boyfriends of yours who might be carrying a grudge?"

"Uh-uh."

"What about threats? Could your . . . our mother have received one and not told you about it?"

"No way. She'd've told me because she'd want me to be on guard." Robin's frown was accentuated by the light from my flash. "Sharon, d'you think the break-in has something to do with the hit-and-run?"

"Big coincidence if it doesn't. Did the officers you talked with at the hospital give you their cards?"

"Yes."

"Then why don't you call one of them while I make us some coffee?"

Detective Loretta Willson and her partner, Bob Castner, looked tired; both quickly accepted Robin's offer of coffee. Willson, a thin blonde whose body and facial features were all sharp angles, sat on a sofa in the parlor, placing her mug on a table next to an evidence bag containing the bullet the lab techs had dug out of the door frame upstairs. Castner, dark and as round as his partner was angular, leaned against a bookcase, warming his hands on his mug. At a glance from Willson, he set it on the top shelf and took out a notebook.

Willson looked at me and said, "Ms. Blackhawk tells us you saw the intruder."

"Only briefly, and I can't describe him. I think it was a man. Not tall, necessarily, but big-boned, judging from the size of his fingers."

"He fired at you?"

"Toward my flashlight, anyway."

"Why didn't you call nine-one-one as soon as you were aware someone was in the house?"

"By the time I realized he wasn't a member of the household, it was too late; he would've heard me make the call and gotten away. So I tried to get a look at him instead."

"Do you customarily confront intruders when you don't know if they're armed or not?"

"Customarily? No, but . . ." I handed her the business

card I'd tucked into the pocket of my jeans when I dressed. "It was a conditioned reflex."

Willson examined it, held it out to Castner. He raised his eyebrows and said, "That's why the name's familiar. The Diplo-bomber case, right? I read about you in *People*."

The *People* magazine profile haunted me the way a bad judgment call haunts a losing coach after the Super Bowl. I merely nodded.

Willson said to Robin, "What about you, Ms. Blackhawk? You see him?"

"The shot woke me. He was gone before I figured out what was happening."

"You have any idea what he was after? Valuables? Cash?"

"We don't own anything very valuable. And we don't keep much cash on hand."

"What about your mother's legal files?"

"They're locked up in the office."

Willson looked at Castner. "They tampered with?"

He shook his head.

"She keep any files upstairs?" Willson asked Robin.

"I suppose she might. She works in her bedroom late at night. But why would somebody be after them?"

"They could contain information someone wanted to obtain—or suppress. We'll take a look around up there, and then I'd like to get started on all her active cases. Don't worry, Ms. Blackhawk, we'll get this guy. Our unit has a sixty-seven percent clearance rate."

I said, "From the way you're talking, I gather that you agree the break-in is related to the hit-and-run?"

Willson's mouth twitched in irritation. "Ms. McCone, maybe in San Francisco the police share their theories with civilians, but it doesn't work that way in Boise. I'm not even sure why you're here. Is it on business?"

"No."

"And your connection to the Blackhawks is . . . ?"

Robin said, "She's my sister."

". . . My information is that your mother has only two children—yourself and your brother Darcy."

"Sharon's my half sister. My mother put her up for adoption before she married my father. We met for the first time yesterday."

"I see." From Willson's speculative expression, I gathered she found my appearance in Boise as convenient a coincidence to the hit-and-run as I did the break-in.

I said, "This information isn't for public consumption, of course. Saskia Blackhawk didn't know my whereabouts, or that I'd located her. She was run down before we had a chance to meet."

Willson threw me a withering look, but Castner's lips curved up in amusement; he seemed to enjoy someone taking a firm hand with his brusque partner.

"My sister," I added, "is willing to cooperate with your investigation in any way possible. As I am."

Robin nodded, standing up and squaring her slim shoulders. "Let's get started on my mother's files. I've watched enough cop shows to know that time's important in making an arrest. I want you to nail the bastard."

Saskia Blackhawk was an active and committed attorney. She carried a large caseload, ranging from major federal suits such as the Coeur d'Alene fishing rights and the Spirit Lake development to minor pro bono work for individual Indians. She'd consulted, although not argued, on a groundbreaking case concerning Indian trust accounts, in which a federal judge held in contempt Interior Secretary Bruce Babbitt and Treasury Secretary Robert Rubin over their departments' mismanagement of income from native lands, dating back to the 1880s. And just last week she'd taken up the cause of a group of Nez Perce who were being forced by a private college in Lewiston, Idaho, to take out prayer permits in order to worship at a sacred peak in the Seven Devils Mountains, where the school's astronomy department had installed costly telescopes.

When Robin finished summarizing some two dozen files, the sun was slanting in the windows of Saskia's office and the four of us were both exhausted and wired from too much coffee. Castner, the note-taker of the partners, got up and paced around, consulting his pad.

"Okay," he said, "the timber interests in the Coeur d'Alene case are definitely suspect. But I think we can discount the federal trust case; the feds're underhanded as hell, but they don't usually resort to hit-and-run, except on 'The X-Files.' Snake River College?"

Willson yawned widely. "I don't know. Those telescopes're expensive, but I can't see a bunch of academics getting exercised enough to resort to attempted homicide. We assign a low priority to that, and we're still looking at over half those pro bonos and the Spirit Lake thing. You got names, phone numbers?"

"Everything we need."

"Let's go, then, so these people can get some rest."

As soon as the officers were out the door, Robin called the hospital for an update on Saskia's condition. No change, she was told. I urged her to try to sleep, but she decided to go over there and wait till she could talk with Dr. Bishop; she would, she said, feel better being closer to her mom. Would I stay with Darcy? she asked. Reassure him if he woke before she got back? Of course, I told her, although I badly wanted to go along to the hospital.

After she left in my rental car—her keys as yet unfound—I went upstairs and looked in on her—our—brother. He lay on his back, snoring softly, oblivious to the events that had churned around him. Sleep made his face young and vulnerable, in spite of the hardware and purple hair. I hoped that he'd be strong enough to handle the waiting where his mom was concerned. Hoped that if he wasn't, Robin could handle him. And, lacking either, that I'd be strong enough to handle both of them.

4:53 P.M.

"Sharon, wake up."

"Huh?" I swam to the surface slowly. The room was unfamiliar, and I was covered by a blue blanket, but I wasn't in bed. . . .

Oh, right, Darcy's room. I'd sat down in the recliner and must've fallen asleep. Robin had probably found me there and covered me, and now she wanted me to wake up.

"What time is it?"

"Nearly five in the afternoon." Her face came into focus, deeply shadowed and strained.

I struggled to sit up. The bed was rumpled, Darcy gone. "Saskia—is she—"

"No change. But you've got a visitor. A man. He says he's your father."

Austin DeCarlo, here in Boise? At Saskia's house?

I untangled myself from the blanket and stood, experiencing a flash of vertigo. My skin felt tight and tingly—a consequence of too little sleep, too much coffee, and no food.

Robin asked, "Is he your adoptive father, or . . . ?"

"My birth father." I started for the adjoining bathroom.

"Then he's—"

"Give me a minute."

I shut the door against her question, used the facilities, splashed water on my face. In the mirror my skin looked grayish and unhealthy; my hair needed washing. I ran my fingers through it, said, "What the hell," and went back to Robin.

"That man downstairs," she said. "He was my mother's lover?"

"Yes. I located him a few days ago, and he told me where she was living."

"How did he know? I've never seen him before in my life."

"Come downstairs with me, and I'll introduce you."

Austin DeCarlo, clad in a blue business suit and red-and-blue-striped tie, stood in front of the fireplace in the parlor, looking up at the painted elk hide. His manner was formal as he turned toward us.

"Sharon, I came as soon as I heard about Kia. How is she?"

"She's been in a coma since the hit-and-run."

"Did you get to meet her?"

"No." I drew Robin forward. "This is Austin DeCarlo, my father. Robin Blackhawk, my half sister."

DeCarlo extended his hand, but Robin sucked her breath in and backed up, her face hardening. "Austin DeCarlo, the Spirit Lake developer?"

"Yes," I said.

"Why didn't you tell me he was your father?"

"You had enough to deal with, without me dumping that on you. Now that he's here, though—"

"Now that he's here, I'd like to spit in his face!" She glared at DeCarlo. "First you knock up my mother and leave her. Then—"

"Ms. Blackhawk, I realize we aren't meeting under the best of circumstances—"

"Circumstances? Circumstances that *you* created! You're the one, aren't you? The one who tried to kill my mother?"

DeCarlo frowned. "Kill Kia? Why would I—?"

Robin made an enraged sound, half grunt and half scream, and hurled herself at him. Her fists pummeled the air, and then his chest. DeCarlo fended her off, his hands on her shoulders, while I grabbed her from behind.

"Robin, calm down!" I said. "He wouldn't've come here if—"

"He shouldn't've come here at all!" She broke my hold, slamming me against the wall next to the archway. By the time I caught my breath and started after her, she was halfway up the stairs, sobbing harshly. I let her go.

DeCarlo came over to me. "Are you okay?"

I nodded.

"Jesus, what was all that about?"

"Why don't we sit down."

I felt terrible about the whole business. I should have prepared Robin. An oversight, because I was disoriented and tired and surprised Austin was here? Or had I subconsciously pushed the confrontation, hoping to learn something from his reaction? Was my mind really that devious, even when half asleep? Was I really that cruel?

"Exactly why are you here?" I asked him.

"I heard about Kia's accident from my attorney. I thought you might need my support."

His reasoning was preposterous. In forty years he'd made only the one attempt to locate me, and now he was rushing to my side, wanting to be a daddy.

My expression must have given away my thoughts. "All right," he said. "I was presumptuous, but I can't help the way I feel."

"How'd you know where I was?"

"From your office."

I'd called the agency machine last night, left the address and number. "You should've phoned first."

"I realize that now. Why does Robin think I tried to kill Kia?"

I explained the circumstances of the hit-and-run. "The police are looking at everyone in an adversarial relationship to her and her causes. You're a top priority."

"Because of Spirit Lake? That's crazy."

"Is it? Where were you last night, Austin?"

"Oh, come on!"

"Where?"

"With my friend Nicole, making up for leaving her at the restaurant the night you found me."

It made sense, and I wanted to believe him, but . . . "We need to talk about Spirit Lake," I said. "Before the police contact you. Does anyone in Monterey know you're here?"

"My executive assistant, and he won't give out information."

"Good. We can't talk here, though. Why don't you check in to a hotel?"

"I have a reservation at the Grove."

"Then go there, and I'll be along after I smooth things over with Robin."

He nodded and stood. For a moment he hesitated, as if he wanted to say something more, but then he turned and left. I stayed where I was for a few moments before I went upstairs to comfort my half sister.

7:02 P.M.

I walked across the downtown plaza known as the Grove toward the hotel of the same name, dodging rollerbladers whose skates rumbled on the brickwork. Mist from a fountain that sent columns of water high in the air caressed my face. The evening was warmish, and people strolled along or sat at the outdoor tables of the cafés. A young woman with electric green hair and a filmy pink dress twirled a rainbow-striped parasol; she was soon joined by two men dressed in black leather and metal ornaments, whose dye jobs made them look as if they were wearing skunks on their heads. Unlike many cities', Boise's downtown district was far from dead after office hours, and highly entertaining.

Austin DeCarlo's hotel was clearly one of the best in town, and his thirteenth-floor suite had to be their finest. As he settled me on a sofa with a mountain view and poured me a glass of Chardonnay, I reflected on the irony of my situation.

No one in the McCone family had ever possessed the ability to attract much money; my parents and aunts and uncles had pretty much lived hand-to-mouth or on credit. My brothers and sisters and I worked on weekends and during the summers as soon as we were of age, and when I decided to go to college after a two-year stint as a department-store security guard, it was understood that it would be on my own nickel. For years after graduation I paid off student loans while working at low-salaried jobs, and had it not been for a cash reward from a grateful client, I might never have owned a house. A second reward, this one from the federal government, bankrolled my agency's expansion. I was doing well, but out of lifelong habit, I still counted every penny. Now, though, I had a rich father who could buy anything he pleased. Could buy me anything I pleased—as long as I pleased him.

So why didn't it matter to me?

Austin settled into an oversized chair; he'd changed to jeans and a sweater, and his feet were clad in moccasins. He lounged low, stretching out his long legs, a glass of Scotch in hand.

"You get things straightened out with Robin?" he asked.

"Yes. She allowed as how she'd acted out of proportion to the situation. You didn't see her at her best; normally she's quite levelheaded."

"And the brother? What's he like?"

"That's another thing entirely. But I didn't come here to discuss Saskia's family. We need to talk about Spirit Lake. The police will be looking at you as a suspect, both in the hit-and-run and the break-in at the Blackhawk house. They'll gather background on the dispute over the project. They'll gather background on you and your past relationship with Saskia."

"Jesus, I can prove where I was last night—"

"I know that, but the police might contend you were setting up an alibi because you'd hired the hit and the break-in. We need to talk everything over and find a way to diffuse those suspicions."

"You believe me, then."

I didn't know what I believed, but I said, "Yes. Tell me about the project."

"It's an unusual property, with interesting potential. Do you know anything about Modoc County?"

"Very little."

"Well, the Modoc Bioregion actually includes all or part of seven counties: Modoc, Siskiyou, Lassen, Shasta, Tehama, Butte, and Plumas. It's one of the most unspoiled and diverse in the West: contains forest, mountains, high desert, wetlands, and volcanic fields. And it's relatively unsettled: Modoc County has less than eleven thousand population, the others some half million combined. Spirit Lake is alkalai, in the high desert, but to the east it's forestland and to the west the acreage encompasses lava fields that're more spectacular than those of the national monument near Tule Lake."

"This is all very interesting, but what's it got to do—"

"Sorry. I'm enthusiastic about the property, and I digress. Anyway, I've known about the area for a long time, and a few years ago I heard that the lake and acreage were available for purchase from the Department of the Interior. It seemed the perfect place for an exclusive luxury resort. So I bought the land, had surveys done and plans drawn up. But now everything's blocked by this damned lawsuit, and the Modocs're being backed by a powerful consortium of environmentalists."

"Does this consortium have a name?"

"Not that I know of."

"What do you know about them?"

". . . From what my attorney's investigators have been able to find out, they're a group of wealthy philanthropists who want their good deeds to go unpublicized."

"And?"

". . . That's it."

Some investigators. "Okay, who's the spokesperson for the Modocs?"

Austin's lips twisted. "Mr. Jimmy D. Bearpaw. He lives in Sage Rock, the nearest town to the lake. He's a professional shit-disturber, meaning he goes around getting Indians—regardless of their tribe—all fired up about causes. Then he sits back and enjoys the trouble he creates. This . . . consortium has deep pockets, and Jimmy D's burrowed into one of them. He'll do anything they tell him to."

"Shit-disturbing—it's a pattern of behavior with Bearpaw?"

"Yeah, it is. Up in Oregon, over in Nevada. Six, seven 'causes' in the past ten years, and when it's all over, the only person who's benefited is Jimmy D. Gets his name and face in the papers, gets to feel important. And everybody else loses and gets stuck with enormous legal fees." Austin grimaced. "People like him do the Indians more harm than good."

"And people like Saskia?"

"More good than harm. But because she's so well intentioned and dedicated, she can be naive about the likes of Jimmy D. I tried to tell her that last month, and she walked out on me."

"You saw her last month?"

"Yes. I flew up here, invited her to dinner. She refused, but she agreed to a public meeting. Ordinarily she wouldn't've spoken to one of the principals in a suit she was arguing, but I think she was curious as to what kind of man I'd become. I know I was curious about her, and came away very impressed, except for her one blind spot."

Wasn't he full of surprises! "By blind spot, you mean Bearpaw?"

He nodded. "We argued about him, and she blew up. Nobody as high-powered as Kia likes to have her judgment questioned, particularly by a former lover."

A former lover who had abandoned her when she was a pregnant teenager. I was surprised she'd agreed to see him at all. "Did she say anything about me?"

"She asked if I'd ever tried to find you. She hadn't made the effort either, but in the back of her mind she was hoping someday you'd contact her. I wish I'd known then what I know now."

Meaning what? Was he envisioning a happy reunion of our little family, all the hurts and abandonments of the past forgotten? If so, he was the naive one.

"Well," he added, "do you see any way to diffuse the police suspicion?"

"Yes. Get the detectives over here and tell them what you just told me."

"Okay, I will. Then what?"

"Go home to Monterey."

"What about you? Are you staying on here?"

"Probably not. Robin's boyfriend—he's a dentist in Salt Lake—is due to arrive tonight. She'll have the support she needs, and will let me know as soon as there's any change in Saskia's condition. I think I'll fly back to San Francisco tomorrow and then head up to Modoc County."

"Why?"

"I'm curious about the Spirit Lake property and about Jimmy D. Bearpaw. If he's the kind of person you describe, he just may have disturbed some shit here in Boise last night."

*   *   *

Robin had said she planned to go to the hospital to sit with Saskia that evening, and suggested I meet her there. I was now officially a member of the family, vouched for by my half sister, and would finally be able to see, if not speak with, my birth mother. I felt both eager and apprehensive about doing so, a push-pull mechanism volleying my emotions from one extreme to the other, so I decided to delay for a while, on the grounds that there was something I should do first.

In front of the hotel I took out the rental car company's map and located the Eighth Street Marketplace, a short walk across the plaza. Milford's Fish House occupied the northwest corner of the attractive renovated warehouse complex. I walked past its entrance and turned on Eighth as Saskia had, toward a distant line of trees that marked the river. This was an area of small businesses—linen supply, interior design, caterers, auto repair—all closed for the night; in spite of the nearby restaurants and shops, it was relatively deserted. Under a streetlight I stopped and again consulted the map. Assuming Saskia had not known any shortcuts, she probably would have taken a direct route along Eighth to River Street, and River to Tenth.

Traffic whizzed by me on River, but once I turned in to the short block I felt very isolated. The street was little more than an alley, with a van line's depot and a wholesale florist mart facing each other at its foot, and various other businesses interspersed with parking lots beyond them. I walked toward the far end, past deeply shadowed loading docks, broken glass crunching under my feet.

The street dead-ended a block away at the freeway connector. There were a couple of dark houses surrounded by weedy yards and a few vacant lots littered with debris—an ideal place for a car to idle unobserved until its driver's target appeared. I turned around, scanning my surroundings: chain-link fences barred entrance to the parking lots; one of the security spots above the door of a janitorial supply flickered on and off; the windows of an agricultural consulting firm were covered by bars.

The evening was rapidly cooling, and a wind sprang up from the river, bringing with it the smell of stagnant water. The traffic noise on River Street was muted by the buildings, and the only sound in the alley was the hum of a generator. Last night Saskia had stood approximately where I stood now. What had she been thinking? Who had she expected? What had she thought when she heard the car's engine rev, saw its headlights careening toward her? What had she done? How had she felt?

I shrugged off the useless speculation, began walking back toward the river. Saskia had come here voluntarily, probably without questioning the choice of place. I took out my notebook, began copying down exact names of the businesses. The police would already have canvassed them, looking for some connection to Saskia, but perhaps Robin would know something they'd failed to turn up.

Robin was alone at Saskia's bedside: a wilted, weary figure slumped in a plastic chair. I hesitated in the doorway, and when she felt my presence she motioned me forward. I hung back, my emotional volleyball game at a heated pace. Once I went over to the white-sheeted form hooked up to the IV and monitor, my life would take yet another turn.

Finally Robin got up and came to me. "Are you okay?" she asked.

I shrugged, the urge to flee strong upon me. I could feel familial obligations and demands reaching for me like greedy tentacles. The air in the room seemed thick; I could hardly breathe. Bad enough to have one wildly dysfunctional family, but now I had two—three, if you counted Austin and his father. How was I to meet the expectations of so many people?

As if to reinforce my confusion, Robin said, "I told Darce who you are this afternoon. He's half crazed by jealousy, but he'll get over it."

"Why would he be jealous of me?"

"No rational reason. Darce doesn't even want to share Mom with *me*."

"He's got a lot of problems, hasn't he?"

"Yes, but they're self-created."

"You said he was the all-American kid through high school and college. What changed that, besides the influence of his crowd?"

"Dad's death."

"They were close?"

"The opposite. They always fought, and they had a really bad argument the day Dad had his heart attack. Darce felt guilty, so he got into drugs and now—well, you've seen him."

"Is he in therapy?"

"When he goes, which isn't often. Anyway, enough about him. The doctor had good news for us: Mom's started to drift in and out of the coma. Earlier she was restless, tossed around and muttered stuff that nobody could understand. She's been quiet since I got here, but the doctor says the activity's a very good sign."

Some of my edginess dissipated. "Robin, that's great!"

"Yeah, it is." She nodded at the bed, obviously expecting me to go over there.

I couldn't do it—not in front of Robin. On the one

hand, I felt like an interloper; on the other, I resented having to share such a private moment. Yet how could I ask her to leave—

"Look, Sharon," she said, "I need to call my boyfriend— he's probably at the house by now. Will you stay with Mom for a while?"

"Of course," I said. *Thank you*, I thought. My new sister had understanding and tact beyond her years.

After she left I remained where I was, watching the regular peaks and troughs pulse across Saskia's monitor. The room was cool and quiet; I took deep breaths, and when their calming influence spread through my body, I closed the distance between the door and bed and looked down at her.

A jolt of recognition shot through me, as if someone had flipped a switch and illuminated my life all the way back to my conception. There was no mistaking this was my mother.

Saskia and I resembled each other as strongly as people had said. We had the same oval facial shape, the same high cheekbones, the same tilt of nose. Her eyebrows were like mine, one set a fraction of an inch higher than the other. Her mouth was like mine, and the lines that bracketed it told me this was a woman who laughed hard and often. Looking at her, I had a glimpse of how I'd look in my late fifties, and was not displeased.

Tentatively I reached out and touched Saskia's hand where it lay against the sheet. It was dry and cool, the nails clipped short and unpolished. Again I felt the jolt of recognition, heard myself say her name.

She gave no response.

Tears stung my eyes as I watched her still face. So many years lost, and now—

Suddenly Saskia's lips twitched. Her fingers spasmed on mine, and she moved her head from side to side. Alarmed, I looked for the call button, but before I found it her eyes—brown like mine—were wide open and focused on me.

I blinked and tried to disentangle my fingers from hers. She held on tight, staring fiercely at me. I couldn't tell if she actually saw me or not. Her tongue moved over her dry lips and she said something in a whisper.

I leaned closer. She whispered again.

"I'm sorry, I didn't hear that."

Her eyebrows knitted together, and she seemed to be forcing herself to concentrate. "Find . . ." she said.

"Find?"

". . . Cone . . ."

Cone? McCone? Was she referring to me? "Saskia, I'm—"

"Cone," she said. "Sinner . . ."

Yes, she had to be flashing back to the time she'd become pregnant out of wedlock and later given me up. "It wasn't a sin—"

She tossed her head, extremely agitated now, squeezing her eyes shut. "Find," she muttered.

Then she lapsed into unconsciousness, leaving me holding the frayed ends of a connection that extended back before my birth.

"That's all you know about this consortium of environmentalists?" Hy asked.

I pulled the covers higher around my shoulders so they covered the hand that held the receiver. It was cold in Boise tonight, but Robin—as frugal as I—had turned down the heat before we went to bed.

"That's all Austin could tell me," I said.

"Well, I'll make some calls, see if any of my contacts know of them. Now, what's this about going to Modoc County?"

"I need to check something out. Have you ever been there?"

"Once, a long time ago. Somebody or other was trying to crap up the forestland, and I was there to protest."

"You get arrested?" For years following the untimely death of his wife, environmentalist Julie Spaulding, Hy had managed to get himself incarcerated for unruly behavior during protests in any number of jails across the Western states—his way of dealing with his grief.

"Nope, not in Modoc. Folks up there are pretty mellow. They just laughed at us, called us yarn people."

"Yarn people?"

"You know—sandals, natural foods, back-to-the-land. Politically correct, with no sense of humor."

"None of which applies to you. D'you ever miss it?"

"Getting busted? No."

"I mean the environmental work."

"Well, I still do some fund-raising for Julie's foundation, but as for chaining myself to a tree on a rainy morning before I've even had a cup of coffee? Forget it, McCone. I'm too old for those kind of antics. So when d'you want to go to Modoc?"

"Tomorrow, if you don't need Two-seven-Tango."

"I don't, but it's probably not a good idea to fly."

"Why not?"

"Lots of airport closures up there lately, and it's not easy to get hold of rental cars. You want to keep a low profile, right?"

"Yes."

"Well, you land at one of those small fields in a flashy number like Two-seven-Tango, you'll really be calling attention to yourself. Here's a solution to the problem: I'll pick you up at SFO tomorrow and we'll fly to the ranch, borrow Pete Silvado's truck, and drive it to Modoc. That rattletrap's perfect protective coloration."

Pete Silvado was one of the Paiutes who worked Hy's small sheep ranch; his truck was a rusted-out green Ford of uncertain vintage. "You think he'd loan it to me?"

"To me, in exchange for the use of my Land Rover."

"You want to come along?"

"Why not? I wrapped up that risk analysis for the prospective client this afternoon; now it's up to Dan Kessell to get him to sign on the dotted line."

"Then I'll see you tomorrow morning at SFO."

LISTENING . . .

"*Does this consortium have a name?*"

"*Not that I know of.*"

"*What do you know about them?*"

"*. . . From what my attorney's investigators have been able to find out, they're a group of wealthy philanthropists who want their good deeds to go unpublicized.*"

"*And?*"

"*. . . That's it.*"

*   *   *

"This . . . consortium has deep pockets, and Jimmy D's burrowed into one of them."

I'm getting to the point where I can read you, Austin. Those hesitations before you speak of the consortium tell me you know or suspect more about them than you're telling. But what? And why won't you confide in me? Instead, you sidetracked me onto Jimmy D. Bearpaw, who's probably a minor player in the scenario.

Didn't work, but all the same I'll take a look at Mr. Bearpaw. Could be that the answers to some of my questions lie in Modoc County.

"Find . . ."
"Find?"
". . . Cone . . ."
"Saskia, I'm—"
"Cone. Sinner . . ."

Plenty of silence around those cryptic words. She's referring to me, of course. Knows she's in bad shape and wants to see the child she gave up in case she dies. Only natural for her to have been thinking of me recently. After all, she met with Austin last month for the first time in nearly forty years.

But what's this about a sinner?

Saskia was raised Catholic, Robin told me that. But like me, she rebelled against the Church, left it. Of course, that doesn't mean some vestiges of its teachings aren't lodged in the back of her mind. Lord knows there are plenty in mine.

The Church says it's a sin to bear a child out of wedlock. And that child is said to be born in sin. Maybe she feels she compounded the sin by giving me up. Or . . .

Dammit, neither Saskia's nor Austin's silences are telling me much. I don't really know either of them, so how can I begin to understand?

Saturday

·

SEPTEMBER 16

8:23 A.M.

I stepped out of our tourist-court cabin near Sage Rock, blinking at the sun glare. In front of me laid a wheat-colored meadow dotted with junipers that fell away to cottonwoods and aspens bordering a stream. The aspens' golden leaves flickered like candle flame in the light breeze, and the distant mountain peaks were jagged against a clear blue sky.

We'd arrived so late the previous evening that I'd had no sense of our surroundings. A green neon sign—WILDERNESS LODGE, CABINS FROM $26, VACANCY—had lured us to this first motel. The cabin had its pluses and minuses, namely knotty pine and braided rugs and comfortable chairs on the up side, tepid water and a broken TV and a hard bed on the down. But now I'd awakened and found myself in paradise.

Hy came outside, dressed in jeans and a wool shirt and a scowl. His hair stuck up in wet points. "Electricity's off," he said. "I'll go over to the office, see what's happening."

"Look at this." I motioned at the view.

He glanced at it briefly. "I'll appreciate the scenery more after I can dry my hair and start that coffeemaker."

Grouch, I thought, and went back to contemplating nature.

Hy quickly returned, shaking his head. "They won't come to the door. Office is locked up tight, but I could hear somebody moving around inside. Guess there's nothing they can do about the outage, and they don't want to deal with irate guests."

I shrugged and went to take my shower without getting my hair wet.

"Where to?" Hy asked as we got into Pete Silvado's battered pickup.

I eased over a protruding spring that I'd become uncomfortably intimate with on the drive up and settled onto the seat. "Town. Specifically, the Cattleman's Cafe for breakfast."

"Why there?"

"Because the background check that Mick ran for me on Jimmy D. Bearpaw shows he owns it. If he's there, maybe we can strike up an acquaintance."

"What's our cover story?"

"I'll know after I see Jimmy D."

Sage Rock consisted of one main street lined with businesses and a dozen or so unpaved side roads where trailers and prefab houses sat on small lots. I glanced down them as we drove by, saw trash dumps and defunct cars and trucks, rusted appliances and cast-off furniture. A couple of vans set up on blocks had a canvas canopy strung between them; a kettle barbecue and some folding chairs told me people lived there. The Cattleman's Cafe was at the far end of the business section, flanked by a grocery and a barbershop. The buildings, wooden frame with iron roofs, were badly in need of paint. Before we went inside I stopped at a newspaper dispenser and bought a copy of last Thursday's *Modoc County Record*.

The café was small—six tables along the window wall and a counter with stools facing the cooking area. Sloppily hand-lettered signs were tacked helter-skelter on the walls:

DON'T ASK FOR CREDIT. YOU DON'T DESERVE IT.

ALL OUR ROADKILL GUARANTEED FRESH.

BURGERS COOKED TO SATISFACTION—JIMMY D'S.

NO FRIES SERVED HERE. JIMMY D DON'T LIKE THEM.

YOU GOT A COMPLAINT, TAKE IT OUTSIDE.

"It ought to be called the Attitude Cafe," I told Hy as we sat down at the end of the counter.

A man in a long white apron was flipping eggs on a griddle, his back to us. "Hey, Ed," he called over his shoulder, "you're here pretty late. Got a hangover again?"

"Screw you, Jimmy D," Ed, a diner in mechanic's overalls, said.

Jimmy D. Bearpaw was short and built like a fireplug, but his movements were as quick as a man half his girth. He dashed from the eggs to another griddle covered with frying bacon and sausage, tended to them, then darted back to the eggs and slid them onto plates. His long hair was tied up in a net and his apron smeared with various unwholesome substances. When he turned to send the filled plates skidding along the counter, I saw he was good-looking in a rough-hewn, broken-nosed way. He grinned and made a high sign at a woman who had just come in, and several gold fillings flashed. As he worked, he engaged in a grating monologue that made me wonder why anybody wanted to eat at his establishment.

"Jeez, Ed, you oughta leave the Green Death alone. Ask

Harley, if you don' believe old Jimmy D. I caught him pukin' his guts out behind the Buckhorn last night on account of that swill."

"Screw you, Jimmy D," Ed said.

"Course, then there's Sandy over there. She's gettin' downright chubby from all that sweet wine she puts away. I was checkin' her garbage bin the other day and—whoo-ee!"

Sandy, whoever she was, ignored him.

Jimmy D took off on Ed's wife's equally bad weight and drinking problems as a weary-looking waitress in a T-shirt that read I SURVIVED THE CATTLEMAN'S CAFE came to take our order. Hy stared at me in astonishment as I asked for corned beef hash with fried eggs and toast and a side of biscuits and gravy. After he'd ordered a cheese omelet, he said, "I've never seen you eat a breakfast like that, McCone."

"No? Must be the mountain air. That particular combo just sounded like my idea of heaven."

"Biscuits and gravy? Cholesterol city. And the hash'll be that awful stuff out of a can."

"That's what it's supposed to be for hash and eggs. As for cholesterol, I didn't notice you telling her to hold the home fries. And your cheese'll be Velveeta."

"One person's poison . . ." He sipped coffee, and we listened to Jimmy D complain about the new traffic light that didn't cycle properly.

"Highway department's got its head up its butt, giving us somethin' like that. Where do they think this is, anyway? L. fuckin' A?" The waitress picked up three plates for one of the window tables and he added, "Christ, Angela, you get any slower, I'm gonna have to buy you one of those motorized wheelchairs! You're almost as slow as Ed over there, and that's slower'n a snail. You don' believe Jimmy D, just ask Ed's missus."

Ed, a man of great originality, said, "Screw you, Jimmy D."

As before, Bearpaw ignored him. "Hey, any of you hear about that woman lawyer, Blackhawk, almost got whacked in Boise the other night? The one our Modoc Council got to fight that developer from down south, the one who's tryin' to put a resort on Spirit Lake?"

At last—something interesting.

"Hit-and-run, and you can bet that developer had his greedy paws in it, on the wheel of the car or not. I tell you, things're gettin' ugly, and we all better watch out. Next thing you know, old Jordan Stump or Carleton Westley or yours truly'll end up whacked. Shit, man, any of us who want to see the land left alone is in trouble. You don' believe Jimmy D, just—"

I said, "What's this about putting a resort on Spirit Lake?"

Jimmy D paused in the process of sliding my eggs onto my hash. "You a reporter?"

"Environmentalist. What's going on up here?"

He snapped his fingers and Angela handed him Hy's plate, so he could come along the counter and set them in front of us. "You just passing through?"

"Well, we're not sure. I'm Sharon Ripinsky, and this is my husband Hy. You've probably heard of him: he helped save Tufa Lake, and he's chairman of the Spaulding Foundation."

"Oh, yeah, sure, sure." Jimmy D's expression said he hadn't a clue as to where Tufa Lake was or the function of the foundation. "Your group does good work, man."

"Thanks," Hy said ironically.

"Anyway," I went on, "we drove up from the Bay Area so I could try to trace some relatives I think may live around here. I'm Shoshone, and part of the family migrated over from Idaho in the early nineteen-hundreds. If Hy and I like it here, we might stay."

"Is that a fact? I guess the cost of living down there gets to you after a while."

"Cost of living, traffic, crime, pollution—you name it."

"Well, you've come to God's country. Even our crime rate's down this year—off seven percent for felonies, fourteen for misdemeanors. What's the name of these relatives?"

"Tendoy." I'd already checked the phone book and found none listed.

"Don't know them. What you might do is go see the folks at the Modoc Tribal Council office down the street at the corner of Cottonwood. We're the only Indian organization in town."

"Thanks, I'll try that."

Jimmy D motioned at my copy of the newspaper. "You thinking of looking at houses?"

"At the ads, anyway, to get an idea of prices."

"In a word: cheap. And I just happen to have a house for sale. Nice little place outside of town on a couple of acres. Tell you what: You scope out the area today; I guarantee you'll love it. Then tonight you meet me at the house after I close up here. Around nine, say. I'll show it to you."

I flashed an uncertain glance at Hy. "What d'you think, sweetheart?"

He nearly choked on his coffee. "Well, *baby*, no harm in looking, is there?"

"None at all," Jimmy D said, and began writing directions on a napkin. "You won't regret this, I guarantee it."

The Modoc Council office was in a storefront that had once housed a soda fountain; even the faded ads for sundaes and banana splits remained on the walls, although the stools had been uprooted and the counter was now covered with books and literature. The rest of the room was crammed with bulky, decrepit sofas and chairs. A white-haired man with a squared-off jaw and downturned lips was talking on the phone when we came inside.

"Uh-huh . . . Yeah . . . Look, Jenny, dammit, you know you gotta get out of there. I'll help you pack up the kids and I'll drive you to that shelter in Alturas the welfare lady told you about. . . . No, Ron won't be able to bother you there. . . . I know, because that's what the lady said, and she— Goddamn it, Jenny, don't hang up— Shit!"

He slammed the receiver into its cradle and scowled at it, then looked up at us with defeated eyes. "My grand-daughter's drunken husband beat her up for the third time this month, and she's *still* afraid to leave him. Thinks she's afraid now, wait till he takes it into his head to kill her."

I said, "Maybe you should ask the social worker to talk to her again."

"She's talked till she can't talk no more. Nothing's gonna change till Jenny decides to change it, and I hope to God that happens soon. I'm Jordan Stump. What can I do for you folks?"

I told him my cover story about looking for relatives and said Jimmy D. Bearpaw had suggested I come here. Jordan Stump got to his feet slowly and motioned for us to be seated on a lumpy plaid couch. As he followed and lowered himself onto a matching armchair, he limped and winced in pain.

He adjusted the pillow behind his back. "Not a good day."

"Arthritis?"

"Combination of things. When I was young, I fancied myself a bull rider. Didn't take long for a big Brahma to prove I wasn't. Now, you say your people're called Tendoy?"

"Yes. I heard they came over from Idaho in the early nineteen-hundreds."

"Well, I'll get my spies working on it, see what they can find out. Most of them're older than God, so there's a good chance somebody might remember your family. Afraid I can't help you myself; I've only lived here a few years, like most of our tribal council members."

"I thought this was the Modocs' native territory."

"It is, but . . . I guess you're not familiar with our history."

I shook my head and waited.

"Well, we were never a tribe in the usual way, just separate little bands hunting and foraging over the same few thousand square miles. Only eight hundred people, all told, when the white men came. They ruined our hunting, scared the game away. So we massacred some of them, and they massacred some of us. The kind of dispute where in the end nobody knows who started it. Finally in 1864, we negotiated a treaty that removed us to a Klamath reserve up in Oregon. You ever hear of the Modoc War?"

"No," I said.

"Yes," Hy said.

Jordan Stump waggled his finger at me. "And he's not even Indian."

"He probably paid more attention in California history class than I did."

"Well, the conditions up at the Klamath reserve were miserable. A Modoc leader named Captain Jack—real name Kientepoos—rebelled, and twice he led a band of three hundred and some back to the Lost River over by Tule Lake. The second time, in April in 1870, things worked out okay, and they stayed there for about two years before the government sent troops in to force them back to Klamath. You ever been to the Lava Beds National Monument?"

"No," I said.

"Once," Hy said.

"Go again, and take her. She's badly in need of education. The lava beds were the battlefield for the Modoc War. Our people knew them, could slip in and out through the chasms and fissures, hide in the caves and tubes. There's a big pit out there at the southern end of Tule Lake called Captain Jack's Stronghold; it was their base camp. The government soldiers didn't stand a chance in that kind of territory."

Hy said, "A pretty costly war, wasn't it?"

Jordan Stump nodded. "Costly for the government in terms of both life and money. Costlier to us, because we lost everything. We could outfight them, but there was dissension in the ranks. When the government proposed peace talks, a group of militant Modocs kept after Captain Jack until he agreed that if the representatives didn't meet their demands, they should be killed. And that's just what happened. The assassinations were the beginning of the end for us. Captain Jack and three other leaders were tried and hanged, and the remaining hundred and fifty-three of our people were shipped off to Oklahoma Territory in boxcars like cattle. That's where I was born and raised—Ottawa County, Oklahoma."

I said, "But now you've moved here. Why?"

"If you look to yourself, you ought to be able to answer that question. You're a relatively young woman, but already you're searching for your roots. That urge gets even stronger as you age. I was sixty-seven when I heard about this tribal council. It was formed by some young Modocs whose grandparents went back to the Klamath reserve when the government finally allowed it in 1909. Young people are interested in learning about and preserving the old ways, not like in my day when we all wanted to be white. They decided to move back to their ancestral territory, reunite the tribe. And they wanted elders who had a sense of history to join in."

"And now I hear there's a developer who wants to bar your access to your sacred lands at Spirit Lake," I said.

"Jimmy D tell you about that?"

"Yes. He says you're suing for title to the land. Who's bankrolling the suit?"

"Jimmy D's the only one who knows, and he won't say."

"Why not?"

"He claims it's a condition of their backing us." Jordan Stump frowned. "I myself prefer to know who I'm dealing with, but if that's the way they want it, that's the way it'll be. We need whatever help we can get. When I packed up my granddaughter and her family and came up here, Sage Rock was practically a ghost town. In a lot of ways it's still not so great. There's nothing for the young people to do, so they drink and get in trouble, and it's hard on young families like Jenny's. We've got a lot of work ahead of us, but in time we'll have a community center and a museum, powwows and other cultural events. And then we'll have proved to the world that the Modocs can be a tribe, that even the U.S. government couldn't destroy us."

Jordan Stump's words would have been inspiring had there not been a hollowness behind them. I glanced at Hy, saw he sensed it too.

The Modocs had twice been removed from their lands; they'd returned to find them a place where alcoholism, spousal and child abuse, crime, and poverty flourished. And now they perceived a new threat in the form of Austin De-Carlo's development plans.

The dream that Jordan Stump and the others had traveled thousands of miles to fulfill was dying—and he knew it.

After we left Stump, we went back to the Wilderness Lodge to make some phone calls. The electricity had been restored, the room made up, and a few messages slipped under our door. Hy's were from a couple of his contacts with environmental organizations, and when he returned the calls, the news wasn't helpful: no one had heard of a wealthy, secretive consortium that was intent on saving the Spirit Lake area.

I went to the phone and began making calls of my own: to Mick, who was only now starting on a series of checks I'd asked him to run; to my home machine, where none of the messages were of any consequence; to Robin, who reported a reversal of Saskia's condition.

"She's back to the way she was right after the accident," she said. "No more activity of any sort."

Damn! "How're you holding up?"

"I'm okay. Evan's been great; I can lean on him." Evan was her boyfriend from Salt Lake.

"How about Darcy?"

"Not so good. Evan's been spending time with him. He says all Darce wants to do is get stoned and obsess about how Mom never loved either of us. He claims we were just replacements for you."

"That's not true."

"Of course it's not, but Darce has never been a rational thinker. I don't know what I'll do with him if Mom doesn't make it; he'll really be a mess."

"We'll deal with him. Together."

"Thanks, Sharon. I needed to hear you say that."

By the time I ended the call, I felt both depressed and helpless. Hy sensed it and stood up. "Come on, McCone. We're out of here."

"Where're we going?"

"To check out the land that's caused all this commotion."

1:10 P.M.

The land was posted and fenced, the main access road gated but not locked. I said to Hy, "I've got Austin's permission to look over the property," and got out of the truck. After opening the gate so he could drive through, I secured it behind us.

The dirt road dipped and meandered aimlessly, as if it had been graded for no clear purpose. We passed through typical high desert country: red-and-brown rocky hills and sagebrush-carpeted flats with an occasional pine or scrub oak eking out a precarious existence. The sky was pale blue with a streaky cloud layer, and the fall sunlight shone weak and watery. It seemed warmer here than in town. After about ten minutes, we crested a rise and saw Spirit Lake spread on a flat plain below us, shimmering like a mirage that might vanish at any second.

The lake was shaped like an unevenly proportioned figure eight with a land bridge where the loops met; in the center of the larger one a black island limed with bird droppings rose—the tip of a submerged volcanic crater, Hy said. Waterfowl did touch-and-goes or fullstop landings on it, skimmed close to the mirrorlike gray water.

Hy put the truck in neutral and we coasted down to the

pebbled shore and got out. The water was eerily still, and all I could hear were the cries of the birds. "No wonder the Modocs considered it sacred," I said.

"I hope it's not too sacred for us to eat our lunch here. I'm starved."

"So am I."

We spread the picnic we'd bought at the town's small grocery on a ledge of rock overhanging the water. Deviled eggs, salami, provolone, crackers, and pears, washed down with a cheap but palatable wine. A feast. After I finished I lay on my back, feeling the sun-warmth of the rock through my shirt and the breeze on my face.

"Ripinsky, I hope Austin loses the suit."

"Me too."

"If he destroys this place, I don't think I'll be able to deal with him. I've already lost my adoptive father; I may lose both my birth mother and Ma. I don't want to lose him too."

Hy was silent, waiting for me to talk it out. But I had nothing more to say, so after a moment I sat up, helped him collect the remainders of the meal, and we went back to the truck.

"Which way now, McCone?"

"Wherever the road takes us."

"Dammit, that thumping's got to have something to do with the fan belt," Hy said.

"Sounds like."

"This truck! It'd be just our luck to break down out here in the middle of nowhere." He steered it to the side of the road, got out, and raised the hood. I got out too.

"Belt's frayed, all right," he said as he peered under the hood. "Doubt it'll get us back to civilization."

"I thought Pete took good care of this machine."

"He does." Hy leaned in farther. "Well, well. Very interesting. Check this out."

I looked where he pointed. The belt was frayed, yes, but the process had been started by a series of small, clean cuts. "Somebody didn't want us to travel too far."

"Or maybe to get back any too quick."

"Now what?"

"I'll take a look through that lockbox in the bed, see if there's a spare on hand. Chances are there is."

I turned away and started walking along the edge of the road toward where it took an abrupt turn to the west. The soil here was rough, clinkery, with a dusting of pale pumice, volcanic in origin. The lava beds that Austin had told me about must be nearby. Sagebrush and bunchgrass crowded between black outcroppings, and the dried golden flowers of rabbitbrush rustled in the wind. I rounded the curve and stopped, drawing in my breath.

Ahead lay a level plain covered by torturously twisted rock formations, towering domes, and chasms that cut deep into the earth. Under the scrub vegetation and loose cinders, the ground was shiny black and rippled, as if a giant hand had spilled a noxious liquid there; the formations stretched their gnarled limbs toward the sky, as though struggling to pull free. The wind blew colder here, whistling around the distorted shapes and howling in the fissures. Green conifers, red-and-yellow deciduous trees, and the ever-present haze of rabbitbrush stood out in contrast to the relentless black like clowns at a funeral.

I hugged myself, cupped my elbows. In spite of Hy's being just beyond the bend, I felt hideously alone. This might have been a landscape after the end of the world as we knew it; I might have been the sole survivor.

"McCone?"

"Huh?" I didn't know how long I'd been staring at the lifeless vista.

"Where were you?"

"Just . . . thinking."

"About?"

"The lava beds." I motioned. "Austin said they're more impressive than the ones at the national monument."

He studied them for a moment. "Guess so."

Something about the tone of his voice alerted me to his unease. "You feel the way I do."

The sensation they called up in me was unnameable—unless I wanted to say the word *evil*.

"Do you suppose this was once a town?" I asked.

"More like your basic wide place in the road."

Hy had found a spare fan belt in the lockbox, so we'd gone back to the truck and turned toward the northern edge of the lava beds. Ahead was a cluster of falling-down, burned-out structures overrun by vegetation. An ancient, rusted gas pump stood in front of one, the canopy roof of the station collapsed around it. A weathered sign sagged across the facade. On the opposite side of the road loomed a volcanic dome. Corroded metal showed through the dry, dense thicket at its base—an old dumping ground.

I said, "Let's take a look around."

The brand of gas was Calco; I found that out by fingering raised lettering on the pump. I said it aloud, looked questioningly at Hy.

"Pre–World War II brand," he told me. "They went into avgas for the military, were bought out by Getty in the fifties."

"How d'you know these things?"

He shrugged. "Just do."

"So nobody's filled up here since the forties."

"Or earlier."

I pivoted, taking in the rest of the place. A blackened foundation looked as if it had once been part of a residence, and next to it stood a small sagging house without a roof or windows. From another house set at some distance behind a stand of conifers came a persistent banging as the wind blew its door open and shut.

Hy was examining the sign across the gas station's facade. "Must've been a general store," he called. "All I can make out is the word 'bait.' The inside's been gutted, and the walls're covered with graffiti. Hey, here's a recent one: 'Olga gave Brandon head.' "

"Either he was bragging or she was advertising. Wonder what this place was called?"

He went over to the truck, took a map from a side pocket, and spread it on the hood. "No indication of a town around here, but there isn't any reason for a new map to show it. Nobody but kids with spray paint cans has been here for decades."

"Maybe somebody in Sage Rock will be able to tell us. Let's check out that house beyond the pines before we head back there."

The house hadn't deteriorated as much as the others, but its walls were sprayed too. A piece of its corrugated metal roof was missing, its windows had been smashed, and a stovepipe chimney lay corroding on the ground beside it. Hy and I stepped into its gloom, and instantly I was seized by the same feeling I'd had at the lava beds. I glanced at Hy, and he nodded in confirmation.

There were only three small rooms: living room, kitchen,

and bedroom; an outhouse was half collapsed under the trees. A few furnishings remained: broken-down pieces that nobody had considered worth stealing; an old wind-up phonograph was the best of the lot.

Hy went over and examined it. "RCA. My folks had one just like it." He touched the record on the turntable, spun it around. " 'Theme from "*Picnic.*" ' That movie was a big hit in the mid-fifties."

"So this place *was* inhabited after the war."

"This house, anyway."

I went into the kitchen. Remains of plates smashed on the floor, drawers of utensils upended. Empty beer cans lined up on the drainboard of the hand-pump sink. The bedroom was in similar disorder, men's and women's cheap clothing strewn about. Under the bed I found a cardboard suitcase, empty except for the sort of fancy comb women used to hold up their hair; it looked like ivory but was probably plastic.

"So what happened here?" I asked Hy.

He shook his head.

"What happened to the owners? And when?"

"Impossible to say."

The atmosphere in the house was more oppressive now: loneliness and abandonment and more. I couldn't shake the notion that something bad had happened here—so bad that even the passage of decades couldn't eradicate its emotional traces.

"Let's get out of here," I said.

"That little town? Sure I remember it."

Mr. Easley, proprietor of the Wilderness Lodge, was a grizzled old man with a beard that came to a point halfway down his chest; he reminded me of a prospector in an old

black-and-white Western. He seemed pleased to have someone to talk with, and his pale gray eyes sparkled as he served
Hy and me beers in his cozy little room behind the motel
desk.

"You say you were out there today?" he asked.

"Yes," I said, "just looking around."

"That land's fenced and posted. Could've gotten in trouble."

"We were careful. It's not the first time we've done a little trespassing. Right, sweetheart?"

Hy gave me a martyred look before he replied, "Right,
honey."

"Heard you folks're environmentalists."

"Uh-huh." I nodded.

"Sure you're not reporters?"

"You must've been talking to Jimmy D. Bearpaw."

"Yeah. You were all he could talk about when I stopped
by the café for lunch. He was really hoping you were the
press. Likes his publicity, Jimmy D does, and he's counting
on getting plenty with this big lawsuit."

"Well, he's bound to be disappointed in us. I can't write
an English sentence, and my husband here's a pilot."

"Thought pilots were smart."

"Not all of them."

Hy nudged my foot and glared. Mr. Easley raised his eyes
to the ceiling, as if he were suddenly afraid one of the less
intelligent pilots would plunge his aircraft through the roof.

"About the town . . . ?" I said.

"Jimmy D told me you two were thinking of settling
down hereabouts. You're not hoping to buy land up there?"

"No. We heard about the lawsuit and were just curious."

"That's good, because the developer's gonna hang on till

the last dog is hung. If I were you, I wouldn't be too hasty about pulling up stakes and moving here."

"Why not?"

"There's nothing to do, 'less you count playing pool and drinking at the Buckhorn. Nearest movie theater's in Alturas. Nearest city's Reno, and that's a long haul. You folks'd go crazy, after living in the Bay Area."

"I don't know; it all depends on what you like to do. Exploring that ghost town, for instance."

"Oh, right, you were asking about it. Indian town, it was."

"Modoc?"

He shook his head. "Nah, most of them only started moving here a few years ago. Those were Paiutes or Western Shoshones or somesuch. That road through there used to be the route to the fishing and hunting at Clear Lake. Ronny Wapepah, he had the gas station and store, sold bait, tackle, ammo, sandwiches. But then the war came and Ronny joined up, got killed in France. Rest of the folks hung on for a while, some died off, the others left. Now you got nothing but ghosts out there." The old man's face grew melancholy. "Nothing but ghosts here too, but most people don't know it yet."

"What d'you mean?"

"Our old way of life is over. That development's going to go through, lawsuit or not. And that'll bring traffic, people. Won't be any peace up here anymore."

"Maybe it'll perk up the economy."

"Nah, not that kind of clientele. The resort'll have everything they need, from film to fancy restaurants. You won't see any of them driving to town to sample Jimmy D's cooking. Right now we got a good seasonal economy going—fishermen and hunters; none of them care about fancy stuff. But a big development with an airstrip and all, it pollutes and messes with nature. Pretty soon the fishermen and hunters'll go someplace else. And then Sage Rock'll be on its way to being just a memory."

"What about you? What'll you do?"

"Live out my days right here on my Social Security. Suits me fine. But the others, the younger people, they'll be gone."

I said, "Like what happened to that little town. By the way, did it have a name?"

"That town? Well, sure it did. Named after the crater across the road from Ronny Wapepah's gas station. Cinder Cone, it was called."

"Cinder Cone," I said to Hy as I shut the door of our cabin. "I misheard Saskia, thought she was talking about me. But she was actually asking me—or whoever she thought I was—to find the place. Why?"

"Something to do with the lawsuit against Austin, I guess." He stretched out on the bed, yawning. "Maybe Robin knows."

"Right." I went to the phone and dialed the Blackhawk house. "No answer, dammit."

"So why don't you call Austin?"

"I should, but . . ."

"Having a problem accepting him as your father?"

"He's not a very likable man."

"Can't pick your relatives."

"No, but it's easier to accept their faults if they've been around your whole life." I hesitated a moment longer, then dialed Austin's number in Monterey. His taped voice told me to leave a message. "Why aren't people around when you need them?" I complained, breaking the connection and dialing my home number to access the machine. Several recorded voices greeted me—among them John's, Charlene's, and Uncle Jim's. I returned the family calls in the order they'd been made. John wasn't home, but Charlene was—and on a mission.

"Listen," she said, "when're you going to stop all this crazy running around, looking for people who didn't want you in the first place? It's really hurting Ma; she thinks you don't love her anymore. You should at least call her."

"I can't do that."

"Ever?"

"I don't know."

"Shar, I know you're angry because she and Pa lied about your adoption. I'm not too happy about that, either. But they thought they were doing the right thing. They never did anything that wasn't in our best interest."

"That's not what you said when they grounded you for running around with that Hell's Angel."

"I was a *teenager* then! Now that I'm a mother, I can put it into perspective. And that's what you should be doing about this adoption business."

"This really isn't the time to talk about it."

"When will be?"

"When . . . I get some things settled." I hung up quickly. Since her divorce from Ricky and her remarriage to Vic Christiansen, my sister had become wise and serene—qualities I admired but didn't want to contend with at the moment.

Hy sat up, looking at his watch. "It's getting late, McCone, and I'm hungry. What d'you say we hunt up some food?"

"Where? The only place in town is Jimmy D's, and I'd just as soon not see him till our nine o'clock appointment. Listen to him, either."

"Well, on the drive up here I spotted a truck stop on One thirty-nine. It's a ways south, but we've got plenty of time."

"Good, let's eat there. But I need to return one more call first." I dialed Jim and Susan's number in the Gold Country. Jim answered and said they'd been wondering how my search for my birth parents was going. I filled him in briefly, ending with the day's explorations and our discovery of the long-dead town.

"Cinder Cone," he said. "Name's got a familiar ring."

"Have you ever been to Modoc County?"

"No. But I've heard that name. Where? Damn my old-man's memory!"

"Why don't you think about it? Ask Susan. Maybe she'll remember." I gave him the number of the motel.

Jim continued to fret. "Usually my long-term memory's good, even if I do have to write down everything I need to remember on a daily basis."

"Maybe you came across the name recently."

"No, there's a feeling associated with it, like it's something out of the past. Unpleasant feeling, if you want to know the truth."

"Unpleasant in what way?"

"Well, you remember the night you visited us and asked about Fenella's trip to the reservation? Both Suzy and I had the same kind of unpleasant feeling then, but we couldn't pin it down."

"I noticed something made you uncomfortable. Did you figure out what?"

"Not specifically. But after that trip things were different in the family. Fenella changed—went to college, got all caught up in her Indian heritage. Grandma Mary started to fail; she'd always been strong and active, but it was as if Fenella's trip reminded her of things in the past that she couldn't live with. Andy blamed Fenella for Mary's decline and got sort of cold and distant."

"So the feeling you have about Cinder Cone could be related to that trip, too."

"Maybe. You know how you wake from a bad dream and can't remember what it was about, but there's an aura that lingers?"

Altogether too well lately. "Yes."

"Well, that's what hearing the name Cinder Cone did to me."

9:21 P.M.

"You're quiet tonight, McCone."

"What?" I glanced over at Hy from the passenger's seat of the truck. Normally he and I would have shared driving duties, but Pete Silvado, the ranch hand who had loaned it to us, harbored a distrust of women at the wheel and had made Hy promise not to let me drive. That was fine with me; the truck handled like a tank, and this way I had more time to look at the scenery.

Not that there was any scenery to admire at present. The sun had sunk beyond the horizon and a thick cloud cover obscured the moon and stars. The chill on the night air presaged a long, hard winter.

"I said, you're quiet. Guess that humongous chicken-fried steak didn't set too well." For the second time today I'd shamelessly indulged myself.

"The steak was great," I said. "You're the one who should be in pain. Nobody in his right mind orders a Cobb salad at a truck stop called Big Bertha's."

"And I'll never order one again. So what's bothering you?"

"My conversation with Jim. What he said about Cinder Cone having an unpleasant association. Plus the fact that we seem to be driving around in circles. We've passed that bullet-riddled cattle-crossing sign twice now."

"And here I thought I was covering my confusion. Problem is, Jimmy D's map looks like hieroglyphics."

"Let me see it." I turned on the cab light, studied the squiggles and arrows. "I think we were supposed to turn at that other barbed-wire fence a couple of miles back. This road just loops around to the highway."

"I'm aware of that, but the fence you're talking about is on the left; the one on the map's on the right."

"Not if you don't hold it upside down."

". . . Oh."

"Just turn the truck around and let me direct you. And when you see Pete Silvado, you can tell him we'd've been a hell of a lot better off with *me* driving."

Jimmy D had told us that the lane to the house was marked by a For Sale sign; now that we were on the right road, we found it easily. Hy turned the truck and we followed a dirt track through a stand of pines. The headlight beams picked out tall weeds in the strip between the tire ruts; they brushed the undercarriage, caught in the wheel wells.

"Place probably hasn't been lived in for years," he said.

"And now Jimmy D thinks he's found a pair of city slickers who'll pay an inflated price for it."

The track ended in a clearing where a dilapidated swing set sat on a gopher-mounded lawn. The small prefab house was tucked under the branches of a live oak, and a metal shed stood a few yards away, ivy-covered firewood stacked against it. A white Ford pickup with a bumper sticker saying EAT AT THE CATTLEMAN'S CAFE—OR ELSE! was parked in front. Both the house and the shed were dark.

Hy braked next to the pickup and looked at me, raising his eyebrows. "So where is he?"

"Maybe the electricity's turned off." I started to get out, but Hy's hand stayed me. "What?"

"I don't like this. Could be a setup."

"Why? As far as he knows, we're exactly who we said we are."

"Maybe Jimmy's smarter than he looks. If he's connected you with Austin . . ."

"Right. And then there's the matter of that cut fan belt." I studied the house in the headlight beams; its windows were covered by shades, but I saw no motion, no one watching surreptitiously from within. The shed's door was padlocked, a heavy chain securing an oversized hasp. Something moved beyond it, and I tensed; then a doe stepped out, eyes glowing red in the light. Momentarily it froze, then whirled and ran into the pines.

Hy shut the engine off and took the key from the ignition. Reached across me and unlocked the glove box where he'd put his .45. Sometimes the constant presence of the gun—for which he didn't have a carry permit—irked me. But not tonight, not in this dark and deserted place.

While he checked the load, I reached up, popped the cover from the cab light, and unscrewed the bulb. If we'd driven into a trap, we wouldn't make easy targets.

We slipped from the truck, Hy holding the .45 in both hands and sweeping the surrounding area. I ran in a crouch to the house and leaned against the wall, listening. Nothing but the distant howl of a coyote. After a moment Hy followed.

I went to the door and tried the knob; it turned, and I threw it open. Dark and silent in there. The hairs on the back of my neck prickled. The air inside was warm from being pent-up in the heat of the day; nothing moved or breathed, but a strong, familiar odor came to me. "Whiskey," I said. "Bourbon."

"Maybe he's passed out."

"Then he must've started early. We were supposed to be here at nine, and we're only thirty minutes late."

"Well, let's go inside, check it out." When I frowned at him, Hy added, "The man asked us here so he could show us the house. He wasn't around, the door was open, so we took a look without him."

I nodded, reached inside, found a light switch. It turned on an overhead fixture covered by a bamboo shade. The room was about nine-by-twelve, sparsely furnished with a pair of low chairs that looked like old car seats. A black-and-gold Formica breakfast bar separated it from a galley kitchen. A half-full tumbler of amber liquid sat on it, and a denim jacket was draped over its end. I started inside, but Hy moved past me, checking out the room and disappearing into a short hallway that opened to the rear of the structure. When he came back he stuck the .45 in his belt and said, "Nobody. Bedrooms aren't even furnished."

I went to the bar and smelled the glass. Bourbon, but not enough to cause such a strong odor. Then I spotted the quart bottle lying on the matted blue shag carpet; the liquor had soaked into its tangled fibers.

"So what's happened to Jimmy, McCone?" Hy said.

"We were late, he started drinking, and then wandered off to answer a call of nature?"

"Maybe. Toilet's busted into two pieces."

"But why didn't he pick up his bottle before so much spilled? Or come back when he heard us drive in? Sound carries out here in the country."

"Yeah."

I went over and checked the jacket's pockets. Nothing but a handful of crumpled receipts and papers. I smoothed the pieces of paper out: two shopping lists and a single phone number in the 408 area code, all scribbled in what looked to be Jimmy's hand.

Monterey was in the 408 area. Quickly I ran Austin's home and office numbers through my memory. No, it was neither of them. I pulled my cellular from my bag and punched in the number. No service. Cell sites were few and far between here.

I motioned to Hy and we went outside to take a look around.

From the rust on the shed's cabin and padlock, no one had entered it for years. I found a corner where the ivy had forced the metal apart, pried it, and used my flashlight to look inside. A tractor-type mower, some tools, a few gallon cans of paint. Hy was inside Jimmy's truck when I returned.

"His insurance card's expired, and he eats a lot of Dove Bars," he called. "Engine's cooling, but I'd say it's been driven within the last hour. I don't know about you, McCone, but the situation here doesn't look good to me."

"To you and me, it doesn't. But if we report it to the sheriff's department, they'll see it differently. Jimmy's an adult, and he's got a reputation around here—probably not a good one. They'll tell us he got drunk and went off some-place; they'll say we should wait till he turns up at the café tomorrow morning, hungover and more abrasive than ever."

"So I guess we'll go back to town and do just that."

A message for Hy had been slipped under our cabin door: "Call Gage Renshaw."

Gage Renshaw: my old nemesis, who once had hired me to find Hy so he could kill him. Now his partner, along with Dan Kessell, in the international security firm. The relationship among the three of them—four, if you counted me—would never be easy, but over the years we'd developed a workable arrangement. RKI often sent business my way, and Hy's association with them allowed him to draw a percentage of the firm's considerable profits for very little work, while utilizing their resources for his human-rights projects. But when they did need his services, the price was potentially high; the situations at which he excelled were always dangerous.

For a moment after he showed me the message slip I stood by the cabin door. Then, when he went to return the call, I escaped to the bathroom, where I splashed cold water on my face and tried to adapt to this shift in plans. I came back as Hy hung up the phone; his body was tensed, brow furrowed in concentration. Already he'd moved far from this room—and from me.

"Pete Silvado's gonna have to get used to a woman driving that truck," he said when he noticed me. "CEO of one of our big multinationals was snatched this afternoon. Gage is sending one of our planes to pick me up at Newell, over by Tule Lake."

I wanted to ask where the CEO had been snatched, where Hy was going, but I knew better. Chances were that he himself didn't know as yet. Gage and Dan passed on sensitive information only if and when a person needed to know—even if that person was their partner and best troubleshooter.

I asked, "How long do we have?"

"Couple of hours."

Not long enough to say all the things we needed to say,

should this job go wrong in some horrible way. Except that we never did put those things into words—our way of wrapping ourselves in the illusion of normalcy.

I smiled at him. "That's time enough."

Sunday

·

SEPTEMBER 17

7:21 A.M.

The phone woke me, but when I fumbled the receiver to my ear, I heard only a dial tone. As soon as I replaced it, the ringing sounded again and I identified it for what it was: the call of a mockingbird, probably perched in the leathery-leaved manzanita bushes that crowded up against the cabin walls. Now it segued into more of its repertoire, the shrill whistle Mr. Easley used to call his little terrier.

The bed felt empty and cold without Hy there, more so because I still carried the tactile memory of his hands and body on mine. I reached tentatively outside the covers, found the air was frigid; I'd neglected to turn up the heat when I returned late last night from dropping him at Newell. After lying there for around ten minutes more, I rushed to make coffee and get into the shower. Then I dressed except for my shoes, grabbed a cup and took it back to bed to sip while I made my morning calls.

First the Cattleman's Cafe. Angela, the waitress, answered. When I asked for Jimmy, she said, "He ain't here, and I'm havin' a devil of a time findin' a replacement cook to help me get the breakfasts out. Who's this?"

"Sharon . . . Ripinsky. He was supposed to show my husband and me a house last night. His truck was there, but we didn't see him."

"Oh, shit. What's he got himself into now?"

"To tell you the truth, we were kind of worried. That remark he made about him or a couple of other people getting whacked—"

"That was just some of Jimmy's bullshit. Ain't nobody gonna whack him, except for his bad cookin'." Someone called out in the background. "Hold your horses, Al." To me she added, "This was the house off County Road Thirty?"

"Right."

"Well, one of the fellas who's in here now lives out that way. I'll ask him to swing by. Jimmy likes his sauce and he likes to wander. Ten to one he got drunk, forgot all about you folks, and took a stroll. I hope to Christ he isn't laying around in a ditch someplace."

Which was more or less what I'd predicted the sheriff's deputies would have said, had we reported him missing.

After I hung up, I went over the events of the night before and remembered the 408 area code number on the piece of paper I'd found in Jimmy's jacket. My cell phone didn't work here in Sage Rock, either, but it displayed the 408 number, the last one I'd dialed. I called it again on the cabin's phone and got a recording that said Agribusiness's hours were from nine to five, Monday through Friday. The firm's name sounded vaguely familiar, but I couldn't place it.

It was too early to call most people on a Sunday, but at least one individual on my mental list was used to me bothering him at odd hours. I dialed Mick's condo, heard Keim groan at the sound of my voice.

"It's *her*," she said to my nephew.

"Okay, that's it!" he exclaimed. "Let's order the T-shirts tomorrow. What d'you think? Ten dozen?"

"Try a *hundred* dozen." Keim's voice was muffled now, as if she'd handed him the receiver and put a pillow over her head.

"Where the hell are you?" Mick growled at me. "Some time warp?"

"Nope. Those checks I asked you to run—"

"Sorry, I was working overtime on that case Ted assigned to me. One of Glenn Solomon's. He—Glenn—is upset you're not handling it personally."

"When you talk to him, tell him I'll take him to lunch and explain when I get back. But those checks for me—can you run them today?"

"Sure, if you want Sweet Charlotte here to kill me. We've got plans."

"Tell her I'll make it up to the two of you—dinner at whatever the new hot spot is."

"Deal." An appeal to Mick was sure to succeed if it involved food.

"Run them after you make a couple of more-important checks. I'll give you the details on those."

"But you won't tell me why you need them done."

"What does that mean?"

"Mom called. I had to learn from her that you're adopted. You could've let me in on the secret yourself."

"I'm sorry. I should have, but I thought you had enough to handle, what with Pa dying."

"And I thought you'd agreed a long time ago to treat me like a grownup."

"I said I was sorry."

"Well, you'd better be. And you'd better tell me the whole story when you get back to town. Now what about these checks?"

"I need more information on Jimmy D. Bearpaw. Exactly who he is. What's his role in the Modoc Tribal Council? Does he have a criminal record? Where was he born? If not in Modoc County, when did he come here? And anything else you can turn up."

"Check."

"Next I need information on a town up here that turned into a ghost town in the fifties: Cinder Cone. Who lived there, when they left, who the land belonged to before it was bought by the Department of the Interior."

"I'll see what I can find, call you back this afternoon."

"Thanks, Mick."

It was an hour later in Boise. I called the Blackhawk house, got Robin. "You still in Modoc County?" she asked.

"Yes. How's Saskia?"

"Better. She's having moments of lucidity, and last night she recognized me. When're you coming back?"

"As soon as I can. Is Darcy okay?"

"Darce is . . . Darce."

Which meant he was still obsessing. "Have the police made any headway on the case?"

"Not that they're willing to discuss with me."

"Maybe I should talk with them. I speak their language."

"Well, if you do, call Detective Castner. Willson doesn't like private investigators, but he's impressed with you because you were written up in *People*."

The average American constantly amazes me: you can do a thousand good deeds, plus discover the cure for cancer, but nobody's impressed unless you get your face in a magazine or on TV.

"I'll try that. Robin, does the name Cinder Cone mean anything to you?"

"No. What is it?"

"Just a town. When Saskia's able to answer questions, you might ask her about it."

"Why don't you come ask her yourself? She's going to want to see you."

"And I want to see her. Let me wrap up things here, and I'll be there."

I ended the call, tried Detective Castner, left a message. Then I took another cup of coffee out onto the porch to sit in the warming sun. A woodpecker was tapping industriously at a nearby ponderosa pine; I wondered how such a small bird could make so much of a racket. The tree's butterscotch scent put me in mind of food—

The phone rang. I went inside and picked up. Uncle Jim. "You've been chatting up a storm this morning," he said.

"And you must've remembered something about that town."

"You bet I have: an argument between Fenella and Katie. I'm getting old for sure, otherwise I'd've remembered right off the bat. It was the only time I ever heard them fight."

"Tell me about it."

"Was the year Kennedy was shot. August or September. I'd stopped by the house to see Andy. He was in the garage, as usual, and to get there I had to pass under the kitchen window. Fenella and Katie were in there, talking loud. Katie was telling Fenella it wasn't right to take the money, even if it was for somebody else. And Fenella said yes, it was right, considering what the girl had gone through."

"What girl?"

"Neither of them named her. Anyway, Katie told Fenella, 'It's never right, not under those circumstances.' And Fenella really got mad then. She said, 'If you'd been at Cinder Cone, you'd think differently.' But when Katie asked her what Cinder Cone was, Fenella got quiet, told her to forget she ever mentioned it. Your mother said Fenella was keeping too many secrets, and she and Andy were sick and tired of it. Then Fenella stormed out of the house and didn't come back till Thanksgiving, when your folks gave her a very chilly reception." He paused. "Sharon, whatever this town was to Fenella, it's important. Like I said, it was the one and only time I heard her and Katie go at it that way."

It wasn't right to take the money, even if it was for somebody else.

I remembered the deposits into Fenella's bank account and the checks in the same amount written to Saskia Hunter. Checks whose dates roughly coincided with the start of a new college semester. My aunt had put my birth mother through school—using someone else's money.

If you'd been at Cinder Cone, you'd think differently.

Something bad had happened in that little town—something involving Fenella and Saskia.

Katie said, "It's never right, not under those circumstances."

Not right under what circumstances?

Blackmail?

Fenella was blackmailing someone over what happened at Cinder Cone?

Who?

But Fenella, a blackmailer? Saskia, a willing recipient of the proceeds? No, it wasn't right.

If you'd been at Cinder Cone, you'd think differently.

Maybe I would.

9:47 A.M.

The Modoc Tribal Council's storefront was open, and a youngish man in a cowboy hat with a long feather plume and a silver band was hunched over a laptop at the desk. When I asked for Jordan Stump, he said, "Not here today. He had to drive his granddaughter and her kids to Alturas."

So she'd decided to leave her abusive husband after all.

"I'm Carleton Westley," the man added. "Can I help you with something?"

I explained that Stump had volunteered to ask about my relatives, and Carleton Westley said, "Oh, yeah, he left a note for you." He rummaged through the papers on the desk and held it out to me.

As I'd expected, the note said no one knew of any Tendoys in the area. I pocketed it and got down to the real reason I was there. "Do you know Jimmy D. Bearpaw?"

"Sure, everybody does. You looking for him?"

"Yes. He was supposed to show my husband and me his house off County Road Thirty last night, but he never turned up. Have you seen him?"

"Not since the last time I had lunch at the café, maybe two days ago."

"We're kind of worried about him."

"How come? Jimmy ain't terribly reliable; he probably forgot."

"That's what Angela said, but yesterday Jimmy was talking about some woman lawyer who almost got killed. He said he, you, and Jordan Stump might be next."

"Oh, horseshit! Excuse me, ma'am. But what does he think? Some developer in a suit's gonna show up here and take us all out with an Uzi? That was an accident, what happened to Mrs. Blackhawk."

"Maybe not."

Westley frowned at me. "Don't tell me you're like Jimmy, seeing a conspiracy behind every tree."

I shrugged.

"Jimmy's problem is he gets too many channels on his satellite dish. Did Jordan look scared? Do I? Hell, no. We're not important enough to kill. If that developer's got a murderous side, he'll go after our backers—if he can even find out who they are. And I don't see how that's possible, since *we* can't. Besides, you know what? We're gonna lose the friggin' suit. Modocs always get the short end of the stick."

"Whose idea was it to sue?"

Carleton Westley pushed back his chair and propped imitation snakeskin boots on the corner of the desk. "Jimmy's, of course. Like everything else."

"What else?"

"Well, who'd you think was behind the Modocs coming back here? Jimmy. Who sent the letters asking people like Jordan and me to move all the way from Oklahoma? Jimmy. You know why I came?"

"Why?"

"Because Jimmy said land was cheap here. I thought I'd buy me a ranch, raise some cattle. The tribal council promised to help out with loans, that kind of thing." His mouth twisted in disgust.

"So what happened?"

"Until he put the rest of us to work, the tribal council *was* Jimmy D. Period. He don't know nothing about loans. Plus this is California. Land's cheap here in the north counties compared to other parts of the state, but it's still way too expensive. So now I'm doing the same thing I did in Oklahoma, which is pretty much anything anybody'll hire me for. This month it's driving the tow truck for Vern's Garage."

"You going to stay?"

"Who knows? Being here on my ancestors' land kind of appeals to me, even though I don't know much about the Modocs yet. For a while I thought things'd get better after that resort went in—that it'd create jobs for us. But then Jimmy had to go and decide to sue the developer. We're gonna lose, and not a single Modoc'll ever be hired there."

"Saskia Blackhawk's got a good reputation as an attorney. Maybe you'll win."

"Our luck, she'll die on account of this accident, and we'll never even go to court. Anyway, she probably lied about our chances. You know how it goes: lawyers, developers, politicians. Indian or not, they're all alike. Lie to us every day of the week."

Jimmy D still hadn't surfaced by the end of the lunch shift, and the man Angela had sent to the house off County Road 30 reported that his truck was gone. "I'm worried," the waitress told me, "and I suppose I oughta go to the sheriff, but if Jimmy's just off on one of his binges, he'll have my ass when he comes back and finds out I've sicced the law on him. Besides, the deputy'd probably laugh me outta the substation."

"Why? A missing man isn't a laughing matter."

"Well, Jimmy likes his whiskey, and he's been known to drop outta sight before."

"All the same, somebody should do something about this."

"I'll think on it. I don't want to cross Jimmy. He's mean as a snake and twice as poisonous."

*　　*　　*

The phone was ringing when I got back to the cabin. Mick, with the results of his checks.

"Pretty slim pickings, Shar. Sunday's a bad day for this kind of thing; I can't get hold of most of my contacts."

"Well, give me what you have."

"Bearpaw was born June seventh, 1946, in Alturas. Parents were Vida Warren and Travis Bearpaw. County property records show they owned land on Sky Road."

I unfolded my map and began looking for it. "Go on."

"The only other record for the parents is their death certificates—Travis in Alturas, December of 'eighty-seven, Vida in Salinas, August of 'ninety-two."

I placed my finger on Sky Road; it wasn't far from Cinder Cone. "What about a criminal record for Jimmy?"

"It exists, but isn't much of one. I asked your friend Adah at SFPD to run his name through CJIS. Mostly it's DUIs and D and Ds. Did some time in Monterey County jail for petty theft in 'ninety-one. I checked property records down there—nothing. He's owned the café up there since 'ninety-two."

"No marriages or divorces?"

"None that I could find."

"So we don't know if he's got children."

"Uh-uh. And I drew another blank on that town, Cinder Cone. It doesn't show on any maps, past or present."

I sighed. "It was only a wide spot, and not much of one at that."

"Anything else you need?"

"A lot, but nothing you can give me."

I was back at the café when it reopened for dinner. "Still no Jimmy?" I asked Angela.

"No, and business is falling off because of that damn

Harry's cooking. Most Sundays, the old folks're pouring in here right away for their early-bird dinners." She held up the carafe of coffee, looked questioningly at me.

I shook my head. "I've been thinking—maybe I can get a line on Jimmy for you."

"Oh yeah? How?"

"Well, I used to know this cop, and he told me that the key to finding a missing person is usually in his background. Have you known Jimmy long?"

"Most of my life. We went to school together. Jimmy quit as soon as he could, joined the Navy. Was stationed someplace down south and stayed there a long time before he came back and bought the café with his mom's life insurance money."

"Where down south?"

She frowned. "I'm not sure. Maybe one of his mom's old cronies could tell you. After she left old man Bearpaw—he was a worse drunk than Jimmy—she moved down there to be near him."

Salinas area, then.

"Was Jimmy in the Navy the whole time he was away?"

"No. After he got out he had a lot of different jobs. Commercial fishing. That he liked till he wrecked his back and had to quit. And he worked for some company that did soil testing for farmers. I guess he must've been a fry cook, too. How else would he've learned?"

"That company that did the soil testing—do you know its name?"

She shook her head.

"Agribusiness? Does that ring a bell?"

"Not really. I don't see how any of this is gonna help you find Jimmy."

"Don't worry. You've steered me in the right direction."

*   *   *

Back at the cabin, I sat down on the porch facing the distant Warner Mountains with a glass of wine in hand and began isolating the facts that bothered me. Examined each one and began asking myself the questions that I should have asked others much earlier. Finally I went inside, took out the picture of Saskia, Fenella, and Austin and studied it.

Yes, there was the thing I'd overlooked.

Quickly I changed to a heavier sweater, grabbed my flight jacket as fortification against the encroaching night, and went to take another look at Cinder Cone.

7:18 P.M.

The dilapidated cluster of buildings was wrapped in shadow. I drove past the gas station and store and parked in the yard of the house beneath the pines. It crouched under their wind-whipped branches, lonely and forlorn. I got out of the truck, located the flashlight at the bottom of my purse, and went inside.

Immediately the feeling of wrongness that I'd experienced yesterday overwhelmed me; it was in the walls, the floors, the air. I stood still, shining my light around and trying to identify its source, but there was nothing to see here except the shell of what had once been a home. As I crossed to the bedroom, I tried to shake off the feeling. It wouldn't shake.

The cardboard suitcase lay under the bed as I'd left it. I pulled it out, raised the lid, removed the hair comb. Neither plastic nor ivory, as I'd originally thought, but buffalo bone. Like the frame of the photograph Elwood Farmer had given me. I took it from my bag and compared the comb to the one Saskia wore in the photo; they were identical.

I put the comb and the picture into my bag and set out to search the house inch by inch, looking for a clue to its owner. Most of its contents had been trashed or stolen, but in a handful of receipts caught behind a kitchen drawer, I found one made out in July of 1956 by Alturas Hardware to Ray Hunter.

Hadn't Austin referred to the favorite uncle whose home he and Saskia had fled as Ray? True, Hunter was a common surname, but given the presence of Saskia's comb—and most likely her suitcase—in this house, it was where they'd come. Why hadn't Austin told me he knew the area because of that visit? And what had happened to Ray Hunter?

Maybe Mr. Easley at the Wilderness Lodge would know.

I hurried out to the truck and started back the way I'd come, but when I passed the volcanic crater across the road from the old gas station, I remembered something I'd seen there the day before. I backed up, pulled the truck close to the crater, and got out, shining my flash around. Its beam highlighted the overgrown dumping ground at its base, and I made out the rusted nose of a truck protruding through the vegetation.

I went over and pushed the vegetation aside; the vines, scrub trees, and sagebrush were brittle, dead or dying. Miscellaneous debris was piled around the truck as if to hide it: boards, the remains of a mattress, an oil drum, some furnishings. Rodents had eaten the stuffing from the mattress, and the oil drum had corroded and leaked—which probably accounted for the vegetation dying. One more hazardous waste site on the planet.

I pulled some of the debris aside and clambered over to

the buried truck. Its license plate was nearly unreadable, but it looked to be the type issued in California in the fifties. I squatted down, ran my finger over the raised date. 1958.

Pulling aside some boards, I went around to the driver's door. It wouldn't open, so I smashed the window, removed most of the glass, and leaned inside. On the steering column was a registration card encased in plastic, as owners used to display them. When I held the flash close to it, I could make out faded letters: RAYMOND T. HUNTER.

Why had he abandoned both his home and a truck that, from the looks of it, had then been relatively new?

Of course. He hadn't.

I backed through the window and straightened. Looked around. My eyes moved to the volcanic dome looming some dozen feet above me. Its mouth wouldn't be large enough to accommodate a vehicle, but . . .

I left the thicket and began climbing the side of the dome, leaning forward on the steep slope, hands braced on the ground. The newly risen moon's light gleamed off patches of rippled obsidian among the rough basalt. I moved slowly, counting each step, breathing at a measured pace. Tried not to think of what I might find or what might have happened here over forty years ago. When I reached the crater's rim I stood for a minute, taking in the clean night air. Then I shone the flashlight beam down inside.

A bottomless spiral of darkness. Black walls, glassy in some places, broken and eroded in others. Moss, lichen, small plants that thrived in dank places. And, farther down, a ledge protruding where part of the crater's wall had caved in. On it I saw a flash of white. Bat droppings?

I lay down on my stomach and extended the arm with the light as far into the pit as I could. Stared at the ledge with squinted eyes. The white blur took on definition, as if a man were lying prone there.

Not a man, a skeleton. Perfectly formed because no predators could disturb it in its volcanic tomb.

I drew back too quickly and my hand smacked into a rock. The flashlight flew from my grip. I watched its beam flare off the crater's walls as it bounced and clattered into the depths.

I was driving past the part of the lava beds where the formations stood the thickest when the truck's left rear tire went flat. It had felt out of alignment all the way to Cinder Cone, and now I knew why. I braked, got out to check it. A nail was driven straight in and had caused a slow leak. Normally I'd have thought little of it, just changed the tire and gone on my way, but in light of my discovery and yesterday's fan-belt incident, it struck me as suspicious.

I crouched next to the tire, looking around. The warped rock formations hulked against the moonlit sky; the chill wind whistled among them. My imagination conjured up a band of fleet-footed Modocs darting across the stubbled plain and vanishing as if the earth had swallowed them. I heard faint sounds as they signaled to their comrades with words and gestures I couldn't comprehend. They were—

Don't fantasize, McCone. Change the tire.

That wasn't going to be easy to accomplish in this darkness, without a flashlight. I went down on one elbow and looked at the braces where the spare was supposed to ride. Empty. I scrambled into the pickup's bed, saw the lockbox was too small to hold a tire. Checked it anyway for a can of that gunk that temporarily inflates one and plugs the leak. No quick fix here, just extra motor oil, spark plugs, miscellaneous parts. Pete Silvado had prepared for every emergency except this one.

Or had someone taken the tire? The same someone who had cut the fan belt and driven the nail in?

I slipped from the bed, watching and listening. Nothing moved except the wind. How far to Sage Rock? Ten miles or so—a long hike, but I'd walked farther. The moon's light was strong enough to show the way. I took my flight jacket from the cab and shrugged it on, removed my wallet from my bag and stuck it in a pocket, leaving the bag on the seat. Then I unlocked the glove box and lifted out Hy's .45. He'd left it with me because he'd be connecting to a commercial overseas flight at SFO and wouldn't be able to take it along. It was heavy, unwieldy, but I maneuvered it into the jacket's deep slash pocket. Much as I disliked carrying a gun I didn't have a permit for, its weight was a comfort.

The road had once been paved, but now it was mainly dirt, pumice, and cinders. I could feel the latter through my shoes, hear them crunch. It was growing colder, the wind gathering strength. I kept to the side of the road, scanning the darkness for someone who might be hidden nearby. Listening for a footfall—

A whining noise, and then a stinging on my left ear. The shot boomed as I dove for the roadside ditch and burrowed deep into the tangled vegetation. Blood dribbled down my temple; the bullet had grazed the tip of my ear.

Jesus, another fraction of an inch and I'd've been dead, same as in Boise!

In the distance a man's voice shouted something unintelligible. I burrowed deeper, hoping he hadn't seen me go into the ditch. The man didn't shout again, and for a while all I heard was the whistle of the wind among the rock formations. Then other sounds whose origins I couldn't place filtered through: a rustling, a crunching. Coming closer.

The gun was useless. It was too dark and the shooter was probably out of range. I had to make a move quickly. But what? And to where?

The lava beds. The Modocs used the ones over by Tule Lake for survival. I can use these.

I began inching up the side of the ditch. The vines around me rustled, but that could have been caused by the wind. My head cleared the top and I took a look around. I couldn't make out anyone, anything, except the twisted forms scattered across the barren plain.

The man yelled again. Again I couldn't make out his words.

I pushed up, scrambled to my feet, and ran.

Another bullet whined, another shot boomed. Gone wide.

I dashed for a formation that was shaped like a gigantic hunchback, slipped around it, and took shelter, panting. The ground gleamed black and shiny; fissures stretched jaggedly in all directions. The man remained silent now. He was out there, stalking me.

One of the fissures zigzagged toward a huge outcropping— jagged hunks of rock hurled high against the sky. I crouched down, followed the crack. Touched the formation and found an arch—the mouth of a cave. I ducked inside.

Cold basalt walls and a sudden respite from the wind. I leaned beside the opening, aware of my rasping breath and the distant drip of water. At first the darkness was total, but gradually I made out details that were highlighted by moonrays coming through cracks in the cave's ceiling: black blobs and dribbles on the walls where the lava had flowed and hardened; white calcium lace where water had dripped and evaporated; a tree root reaching down thirstily from above.

Another shout—close by.

Keep going. In as deep as you can.

The cave's floor sloped steeply. An eroded column divided it like a pillar in a classic building. I slipped around into total darkness, moving with my hands outstretched like a blind woman. They touched smooth glass, rough rock, insubstantial and repellent things like slime and bats' nests. The sound of dripping water came closer, receded. The ceiling sank lower, until I was crawling on my hands and knees. Then it rose again, but the walls narrowed and became a lava tube. I squeezed through its twists and turns.

The floor sloped uphill then, uneven and fissured. My foot lodged in a crack and I twisted my ankle. The blood on my cheek had caked, was sticky under the jacket's collar; my ear throbbed painfully. The air was close and cold; the walls were rimed with tiny icicles.

One step. Another. Stop and listen for sounds. Step, step, listen. On and on for what seemed like hours—

A dead end.

No! I haven't gone far enough.

I pawed frantically for an outlet. Solid rock wall. Dark subterranean trap, so dark I could feel it, hear it, smell it. Taste it, even. Now I knew what hell was like: not fire and brimstone, but complete, endless darkness.

Get a grip, go back, see if you can find another lava tube.

I retraced my steps, fighting back tears of rage and frustration. Then, to my right, I caught a faint glimmer of light. Turned that way, crawling over a two-foot obstruction, and followed this secondary tube to another dead end. Except here there was no ceiling.

I looked up. Stars. The moon. Fresh air. Freedom.

Relief made me lean limply against the cold rock. But not for long.

Where's the shooter?

Gone by now, or keeping a vigil at the cave's mouth. If he'd blundered inside, I'd've heard him. Better to surface now while I still had hours of darkness to protect me.

The wall was smooth and glassy. I took a few steps back, felt around till I found spaces that I could use as hand- and footholds. Started climbing.

A foot, two feet, slip back one. Two feet, three, four—slip all the way to the bottom.

I closed my eyes, trying to convert despair to anger. When I'd built enough heat, I used it as fuel to start climbing again.

Three feet, four feet, rest.

Five feet, six—and my head was level with the ground.

A little more. Slow and careful.

I shoved up, braced my arms on the hardscrabble earth. Rested again, gathering strength. Then I pushed off the wall behind me and rolled onto the surface.

A voice behind me said, "About time. I been waiting for you."

The chill that took hold of me was colder than the wind. I raised up and slewed around—a cornered animal.

Jimmy D. Bearpaw stood over me, legs spread wide, a rifle trained on my head. He was grinning, as if somebody had just complimented him on his bacon and eggs.

"Didn't count on me knowin' these beds like the back of my hand, now, did you?" he said.

I didn't say anything. Tensed, waiting. Feeling the weight of Hy's .45 pulling at my pocket.

"Stand up," Jimmy said.

I stood slowly, trying to counterbalance the gun. But Jimmy noticed. He reached forward, patted the pocket, snagged the .45's butt. "You're well prepared, I'll give you that."

I watched as he tucked my last hope into the waistband of his jeans. He was still grinning. I relaxed slightly. Asked, "Where've you been since last night?"

"Watching you."

"Why'd you disappear from your house before we got there?"

"Idea was to separate you from your husband, but the two of you stuck like glue. I was kinda wasted, anyway, so when you left I knocked off for the night. Where is he, by the way?"

So he thought Hy was still here. "At the lodge, sick. We think it's food poisoning."

He frowned. "Not from my café."

"Truck stop south on the highway. He was better when I left him, though, and by now he'll be worried enough to call the sheriff."

Jimmy shrugged, unconcerned. "What were you doin' out at Cinder Cone?"

"Just poking around. I like ghost towns."

"Bullshit. You're a private dick, come up here from Frisco, and you got somebody real important interested in you. That wasn't no sight-seeing trip."

"Who's this somebody?"

"You can't guess, I'm not tellin'."

"Were you watching me at Cinder Cone?"

"Not up close."

"Why not? You could've grabbed me there."

"I got bad memories of the place. Figured I'd wait, snatch you along the road when the tire went."

"You lived near Cinder Cone when you were a boy. And

your father was an abusive drunk. No wonder you didn't want to go close."

His mouth twitched. "Somebody's been tellin' tales they oughtn't've. I'm gonna kick Angela's tail but good."

"So what happens now? Were you hired to kill me?"

"*Kill* you?" His astonishment seemed genuine.

"You almost did a while ago." I touched my ear, showed him the smear of blood on my neck and fingers.

"Oh, jeez, did I do that? I was just tryin' to get you to stop, is all. You must've got in the way."

"Yeah, I must've. Did I also get in the way in Boise?"

"Boise? Idaho?"

"Boise, Idaho. Saskia Blackhawk's house. Upstairs, in the middle of the night. Three days ago."

The moonlight accentuated his puzzled frown. "Blackhawk? Lady lawyer who was workin' on our case till she got run over? What's she got to do with you?"

"You didn't break into her house and shoot at me?"

"Look, I ain't been to Boise in, what? Ten years."

"And you didn't run her down?"

"Why the hell would I run over my own lawyer?"

"Jimmy, I honestly don't know."

"Well, I ain't no killer. No way, not me!"

"So why all this skulking and chasing?"

"All I'm tryin' to do is make a delivery."

"A delivery?"

"Yeah. Let's go."

His truck was parked off the road about a mile away, tucked in under some scrub oaks. "You do the driving," he said, and motioned me inside. When he was situated in the passenger's seat, Hy's .45 aimed at me, he handed me the keys.

"Where to?" I asked.

"House where you was last night. Don't try any stupid driving tricks, okay? You do, I guarantee you'll come out of it worse off than me."

I started the truck, eased it into gear. "Is this important person who's interested in me at the house?"

"Not yet. Be a while."

"Where's he coming from?"

Jimmy grinned and shook his head. "Did I say it was a he? Turn here, down this road. And don't ask no more questions."

"Here you go." Jimmy D shoved me through the bedroom door. "You want something to eat or drink?"

"No." The thought of either made me want to gag.

"Suit yourself, but I warn you: it'll be hours before you're let outta here."

I didn't reply.

"That door there, it goes into the bathroom. Water's drinkable—"

"Oh, for God's sake, it's not as if you're checking me in to the Four Seasons!"

"Huh?"

"Never mind."

"Whatever. I'll be right out there in the living room, so don' get no ideas about tryin' to escape." He withdrew, locking the door behind him.

The bedroom was empty except for a square of stained and matted gold carpet. I avoided it, sat down on the dusty brown linoleum, my back against the wall. No way was I going to try to escape, even though I could easily have pried open the window. Not with Jimmy only yards away. He had the keys to the truck, two weapons, and was a lousy shot.

I didn't want to chance "getting in the way" of another of his bullets.

LISTENING . . .

"It isn't right to take the money, even if it is for somebody else."

"Yes, it's right, considering what the girl went through."

"It's never right, not under those circumstances."

"If you'd been at Cinder Cone, you'd think differently."

Of course Ma wasn't there—but were *you*, Fenella?

"Fenella was a relative of Saskia's."

"Distant, but she was very fond of her. I've always suspected she had a hand in your adoption. Kia hadn't known her long, but she told me she knew she could always turn to her in an emergency."

Did you, Saskia?

"In 1958 I was traveling around the country with a friend. We were both sick and tired of the Valley, and my father and I hadn't been getting along. He wanted me to learn the fam-

ily business so he could retire and ranch, but I couldn't see myself traveling from office to office to check up on how the plant-tissue analyses were going."

What family business, Austin?

"He worked for some company that did soil testing for farmers."

Agribusiness, the name scrawled on the paper in Jimmy D's?

Agribusiness, the name on the window of the agricultural consulting firm in the alley where Saskia was run down?

"We decided to skip Nevada and go to northern California, where Kia's favorite uncle lived . . . but my father traced us, busted into his house a few days later. Kia wasn't there, she'd gone to the store for some groceries. My father sent me home with his ranch foreman, said he'd take care of things. And . . . I went. I never even got to tell her good-bye."

"Where my father's concerned, I've never been a strong man."

"I've known about the area for a long time, and a few years ago I heard that the lake and acreage were available for purchase from the Department of the Interior. . . . But now everything's blocked by this damned lawsuit, and the Modocs're being backed by a powerful consortium of environmentalists. . . . This . . . consortium has deep pockets, and Jimmy D's

burrowed into one of them. He'll do anything they tell him to."

"I've had a lot of years to think on the subject. A lot of time to plan for the day this might happen. So here's what you're gonna do: get off my ranch and leave my boy alone."

I got off your ranch, Joseph, but I didn't leave your boy alone.

And that was my big mistake.

Monday

·

SEPTEMBER 18

3:35 A.M.

The crunch of tires on the ground outside alerted me; a car's engine shut down and footsteps came toward the house. I remained where I'd been sitting for hours, my back against the wall, not even dozing. I'd sorted through what facts I knew, guessed at those I didn't, and each time come up with the same sad scenario. Now I was ready for this final confrontation.

Voices in the living room, and then the front door slammed. Jimmy's truck coughed, fired up, and drove off into the distance. On the other side of the flimsy door I heard harsh, labored breathing; a shadow bisected the light leaking under it.

Come on. Don't keep me waiting.

The lock turned and the door opened slowly. Joseph De-Carlo's tall figure was silhouetted in the frame, the hallway light turning his thick mane to quicksilver. A sheepskin coat hung loose on his lean body, and in his hand I caught the glint of gunmetal. His head moved from side to side, seeking me out.

I said, "Hello, Grandpa."

A hesitation before he flicked on the overhead. He squinted at me and said, "You know better'n to call me that." Then he blinked; I hadn't washed off the blood from the nick in my ear, and the sight of it was disconcerting even to a tough old man.

"Jimmy D do that to you?" he asked.

I nodded.

He made a disgusted sound, ran his hand over his chin. "Never should've relied on him. He was a piss-poor soil analyst, and he's sure made a mess of things here. Why's everybody who works for me a damn fool?"

"Like your security guy, Tony? Wasn't smart of him to run my mother down in that alley in Boise, right in front of the branch office of a company you own."

He pushed his coat back and shoved the gun—which I now recognized as Hy's .45—into the belt of his jeans. Studied me, probably wondering how much I knew and how much was pure speculation.

"Tony gave you a cloned cell phone," I went on. "You used it to call Saskia from your ranch, said you were in Boise and wanted to talk about me. Asked her to meet you at Agribusiness. But when she got there the only person waiting was Tony, in his stolen car."

A quick twist of DeCarlo's mouth confirmed what I'd only guessed at. "Dumb spic wasn't supposed to hurt her, just scare her. Make her realize what could happen to both of you if she didn't convince you to keep away from my boy."

"And I suppose Tony decided on his own to come after me at Saskia's?"

"That's the way it was, missy. On his own. Didn't consult me at all." DeCarlo stepped back, motioned for me to get up and go into the living room. "Now you and I'll have a talk, settle this situation once and for all."

He indicated I should sit on one of the stools at the breakfast bar, then went around it. He took the gun from his belt and placed it on the counter, his gnarled hand resting on the grip. He'd changed since the first time I saw him: the lines on his leathery face were deeper, his pale eyes hollowed and shadowed. Still, he was a powerful presence—a powerful adversary.

He studied me again with narrowed eyes, this time as if he were trying to place me on the spectrum of creatures he knew; I met his gaze without fear. I didn't doubt he would kill me should he feel it necessary; to Joseph DeCarlo I wasn't human, merely some strange hybrid created by the tainting of his family's blood. But bigotry makes a man stupid and arrogant, allows him to underestimate the object of his hatred. I, on the other hand, wouldn't underestimate him, not for a moment.

"Like I told you at my ranch," he said, "I've had a lot of years to think on this situation. Plenty of time to decide what I'd do if you showed up and tried to claim what you think should be yours."

"I don't want your money. Or Austin's."

"You do. Anybody would. The longer you're exposed to it, the more you'll want it. I realize now I shouldn't've tried to run you off my ranch that day. You're stubborn, got a lot of your mother in you, a lot of those Tendoys, but not much of my son. Austin's a good boy, but he's got no backbone. Can't stand up to anybody—least of all me. That is, he couldn't till you came along and made him swell up with fatherly pride. Since then I've been monitoring the situation real careful."

"Which is how you found out I was in Boise—and here."

"Hell, I couldn't help but know, when he's calling me every day, rubbing it in. Telling me what you're doing, talking about his plans for us being a family. You sure got him believing a load of bullshit, played him like a violin."

"I never—"

"Now, missy, I realize the ante's been upped considerably because my boy's fond of you, and I can't have him thinking I'm the one messed things up. So I'm prepared to offer you plenty to drop out of his life."

"I told you, I don't want your money."

"Everybody wants money. Everybody's got a price. I might have to dicker some with you, but in the end we'll settle— just like I did with your mother."

"You mean, with Fenella McCone."

His face went still, wary. "What did you say?"

"The person you negotiated with was Fenella McCone, a relative Saskia trusted and went to after Cinder Cone."

When I named the town, DeCarlo compressed his lips; his breathing became labored, as it had when he stood outside the closed bedroom door.

Press your advantage.

"I know what happened at Cinder Cone. I found Ray Hunter's skeleton this evening."

His hand convulsed on the butt of the gun. He drew several breaths before he could speak.

"Well, that *does* up the ante."

I didn't bother to respond. "Austin and Ray Hunter were at the house when you and your ranch foreman arrived that day. Saskia had taken the truck she and Austin borrowed into town. You sent Austin away with the foreman, and when my mother got back—"

"You think you know it all, don't you?"

"Most of it. Why don't you tell me the rest?"

Silence.

I said, "You told Austin you'd fixed things, settled money on Saskia, but that wasn't true. Were you planning to kill her and her uncle? Kill an old man and a pregnant teenager?"

Blotches of color appeared on his cheeks. "That's not how it happened, missy. I tried to give her money, but the girl wouldn't listen to reason. She came at me like a wildcat, pure animal—screaming, scratching. Then the old man got into it too."

"So you killed him."

"Shot him in self-defense."

"But you let Saskia go."

"Girl ran out of there, hid someplace."

"And you were afraid she'd come back with the sheriff, so you concealed Ray Hunter's truck and put his body in the crater. Used the other truck to get out of there. When Fenella came to you and said Saskia would keep silent in exchange for money for her education, you thought nobody would ever find out about the murder—and nobody did, or would have, if your son hadn't bought the land to develop as a resort. I suppose you're the consortium that's been funding the Modocs' lawsuit."

"Now why would I do that?"

"Because once development started, there was a good chance Ray Hunter's bones and truck would be found. And then Austin would put it all together."

"He didn't have to. He's known all along what happened there."

Just when I thought there were no further surprises, no further lies.

DeCarlo smiled thinly at my shocked expression. "Right, missy, you *don't* know everything. Austin tracked the girl down a year later, and she must've told him, because he changed after that, wouldn't have anything to do with me for years. But in 'ninety-two I had a heart attack, and he mellowed. At least, I thought he had till he bought that land, started talking about how he was gonna develop it. Trying to force a confession out of me, I guess."

"And did he?"

"Nobody forces anything out of me."

But I have, in a way.

A car was approaching in the distance; I could hear the purr of its motor. Now what?

I said, "It's obvious you care deeply for your son."

"He's my only child. I've spent my life trying to make his life a good one. That's what a father's supposed to do."

"Then for his sake, you've got to put an end to this. Tell your story to the sheriff. You've got mitigating circumstances."

He laughed harshly. "You want me to confess to something that's been over and done with for forty years?"

The car stopped a ways down the drive; DeCarlo seemed not to have heard it.

"It isn't over and done. Austin knows. So do Saskia and I."

He looked down at the gun.

"You can kill me, yes," I said. "But think what that'd do to Austin. You can kill Saskia, and then he'd know you were responsible for both our deaths. Are you prepared to kill your son, too?"

DeCarlo remained as he was, head down.

"Are you prepared to do that?" I asked again. "*Are* you?"

Someone was outside the door now, but DeCarlo still hadn't noticed. He was too inwardly focused.

Slowly he shook his head. Pulled his hand away from the

gun. Hesitated, reached for it again—and picked it up by the barrel. He started to extend it to me—

The door burst open. I expected Jimmy D, but that wasn't who rushed in.

Austin. A shotgun extended in both hands. His eyes were bright and hot; they focused on the weapon his father held, shifted to his face as Joseph straightened and turned toward him, the .45 loose at his side.

"You damned fool," the old man said. "Forty years it took you to stand up to me. And over what?"

Without hesitation, Austin stepped back, pumped a shell into the chamber, and shot his father in the chest.

AFTERMATH

Monday

·

SEPTEMBER 18

Joseph DeCarlo was dead on arrival at Modoc Medical Center in Alturas. I spent the day trying to keep Austin sane and out of jail. There are times when the truth must be repressed so the living can go on living, and this was one of them. Although Austin repeatedly told me he wanted to die, I knew that wasn't true, so I lied and acted confused and eventually muddied the waters enough so the county sheriff's department found it convenient to believe that Austin had killed his father in order to save my life.

I, on the other hand, knew the enormity of the lie. Since the year of my birth Austin had been struggling to gather the courage to stand up to Joseph's contempt, but in that final moment had found not courage but murderous rage. There would be an inquest, and he'd be exonerated, but for the rest of his life he'd have to live with the knowledge that in his love-hate relationship with his father, hate had won.

Thursday

·

SEPTEMBER 21

12:43 P.M.

Austin and I waited in the small terminal building at Newell Airport for our respective charter flights to Monterey and Boise. The weather had turned hot and humid, and the air-conditioning had chosen the occasion to malfunction. I regretted having to turn up the emotional heat as well, but there were questions I needed answered.

"How'd you know where your father was Sunday night?"

Austin kept his gaze averted from me as he replied—a pattern with him over the past days. "He told me that afternoon that he was going to settle things once and for all with you. It sounded too much like what he said at Cinder Cone, so I followed him to the airport and bribed the charter service to take me where he'd gone. He'd rented a car there and asked for directions to Bearpaw's house, and a sob story about a family emergency got me the same."

"Why'd you bring the shotgun along?"

". . . I thought you were in danger. He'd killed before."

And that silence tells me everything.

3:50 P.M.

I stood by Saskia's hospital bed, my eyes on her face—taking in small details, cataloging our similarities and dissimilarities, then trying to look beneath the surface to who this closely related stranger really was. Her eyes did the same.

Neither of us had spoken since we'd said hello. I couldn't imagine what she was feeling, but my response was flat and cold; for days I'd been steeling myself against this meeting, building up my defenses in case of rejection, and now I'd fallen victim to the distance I'd placed between us.

Saskia broke the silence. "When I gave you up, I thought I'd never see you again," she said in her low-pitched voice that was very like my own.

"Until two weeks ago, I didn't know I was adopted."

"Robin told me what you've been through since then—including what happened in Modoc County. How did you know to go there?"

"I didn't. I was curious about the land Austin planned to develop and thought I could pick up a lead to whoever ran you down. But once I was at Cinder Cone, I realized it was important because you mentioned it while you were slipping in and out of the coma."

"I did?"

"Yes. You said, 'cinder,' 'cone,' and 'find.' I guess you wanted somebody to look for your Uncle Ray's body."

"I guess. I've always felt guilty for running away and not seeing that he got a proper burial."

"The way I heard it, you had no choice."

Silence fell again—heavy, uncomfortable. Saskia's face was ashen, blackish shadows under her eyes. I knew I should reserve the tough questions for another time, but they were weighing on me, and I had a right to know.

"Why didn't you report Ray's murder after you escaped Joseph DeCarlo?" I asked.

"I was deathly afraid of him. He was rich, powerful, and I'd seen him shoot my uncle."

"But you couldn't have been that afraid. Otherwise, you'd never have allowed Fenella to blackmail him."

"What?"

"Those checks she wrote you at the beginning of each semester in college and law school—where did you think the money was coming from?"

"She told me it was from your adoptive parents."

"My parents never had that much money to spare in their lives. It came from Joseph DeCarlo."

She shook her head as she absorbed the knowledge.

"Seems Fenella lied to both of us," I said.

Saskia stretched out her arm and took my hand. "Don't blame her, Sharon. She was a very caring woman. Neither of us would be who we are today if it wasn't for her."

"Think of who we might've been to each other if she hadn't told so many lies, kept so many secrets." I wanted to pull away, but instead left my hand where it was—a limp, unfeeling lump of flesh and bone.

Saskia's mouth tensed as she realized I was not only angry with Fenella but with her as well. After a moment she said, "I want to ask your forgiveness. When I gave you up, I thought I was trying to protect you from Joseph DeCarlo, but I suppose it was selfishness as well. I had dreams; I wasn't equipped to raise a child on my own."

"Later on, after those dreams were realized, you never even tried to find me."

"Because Joseph was keeping track of me—and he made sure I knew it."

"What did you think he would do? He didn't want me."

"Exactly. And he would have done his best to turn your . . . Austin against you. That kind of rejection can be devastating to a child or a young woman."

"Sounds like a pretty flimsy excuse to me."

Tears welled up in Saskia's eyes. "Please don't do this, Sharon."

I looked down at our linked hands, incapable of a response. After a minute I said, "There're a few more things I'd like to know."

"Yes?"

"Where were you during your pregnancy?"

"With Fenella and Great-aunt Mary."

"Mary McCone was your great-aunt? That means I'm actually related to my adoptive family, in a weird way."

"Yes."

"Was it an easy birth?"

"No, difficult."

"Well, some things don't change. I've been difficult my whole life. Was I on time?"

"Exactly nine months from the date of your conception."

I nodded. She'd told me what I needed to hear.

Saskia said, "Please don't blame Fenella or your adoptive parents for the lies. If anyone's at fault, I am."

"I don't blame anybody." As I spoke I realized all my anger—at her, at Ma and Pa, at Fenella, at my birth father— was gone. I squeezed her hand, bridging the distance between us.

"So," I said, "what shall I call you?"

"Why not Kia? Most everyone does."

"And what will we be to each other? You're my mother, but . . ."

"But your real mother is the woman who raised you. I

can accept that. But you and I can be friends, can't we? Let's try."

"Of course we can be friends," I said. "In a way, we already are."

9:50 P.M.

I stepped out onto the front porch of the Blackhawk house and breathed in the crisp autumn air. Robin had organized an impromptu barbecue tonight, inviting a few of her friends; now the guests had departed and she'd given me orders not to help her with the cleaning up. I went to the railing, looked through the trees until I found the near-full moon.

Someone moved in the corner of the porch. I turned, saw a tall figure whose hair glistened like cotton candy in the rays from the streetlight.

"Darcy?"

"Yeah." The tip of a cigarette glowed, went out, and I caught the scent of marijuana.

"How come you didn't join the party?" I asked.

"Had to work, and then when I got here you were all having such a good time . . ."

"And you wouldn't've?"

He shrugged.

"You're feeling bad because I saw your mother today."

"*My* mother? Why not *yours*?"

"Because, as Kia and I agreed this afternoon, my real mother is the woman who raised me."

". . . You both agreed?"

"Yes. Just as Robin and I agree that my real sisters and brothers are the ones I was raised with. That doesn't mean your mother and Robin can't be my friends. You too, if you like."

". . . I guess." He ventured a few steps closer to me. "How many brothers and sisters have you got?"

"Two of each."

"What're they like?"

I smiled, realizing I had a surefire way to cement our tentative friendship. "Which horror story would you like to hear first?"

11:27 P.M.

"What'd you say to Darce?" Robin asked. "The two of you were out there laughing, and he was still smiling when he left."

"Oh, I just told him some stories that convinced him he isn't the sorriest excuse for a brother on the planet."

"What kind of stories?"

"About my brothers and sisters."

"Will you tell them to me, too?"

"Now? It's pretty late."

"Why not?" She held up a bottle and two glasses. "We've got wine to finish."

"Okay." I sat down on the old-fashioned porch swing. "I'll start with the time John and Joey rolled me up in the rug. . . ."

LISTENING . . .

"*Will Camphouse is your nephew?*"

"*In a distant way. Our familial relationships aren't as clear-cut as whites', or as formal.*"

"*Does that mean he's related to me too?*"

"*. . . Possibly. There's been so much mixing among the tribes, and other ethnic groups as well, that those connections are very difficult to sort out. If you and Will want to be related, then you should consider yourselves so.*"

"*You speak as if you knew Fenella well, but you say you never met her.*"

"*I didn't, but I feel as though I did. That year I returned to the reserve for Christmas, stayed into January. Talk of your great-aunt was rekindled when she sent presents, as well as two big crates of Florida oranges.*"

"*Can you think of anyone who might be able to tell me more about Fenella's visit?*"

"*Well, there's Agnes Running Horse, my cousin. She lives on the Middle Fork of the Flathead River near Glacier National Park.*"

"*Would she be willing to talk with me?*"

"*I'm sure she will.*"

Something moved under the surface of your gaze, Elwood. Deep, dark, sad. At the time I couldn't put a name to it, but now I think I have.

"Can you tell me who this man is, and where I might find these women?"

"Where'd you get this?"

"From Mr. Farmer. He named the women, but he didn't know the man."

"Yes—Lucy Edmo, Barbara Teton, Susan New Moon, Saskia Hunter. Barbara's dead, breast cancer. Everybody thought Elwood would marry her, but they had a big fight the last time he came home to the reserve, and that was it. Saskia Hunter, I heard she went to college, made something of herself, but I don't know what. I'm surprised Elwood couldn't tell you; they were real good friends."

Yes, Agnes Running Horse, I'm surprised too.

"You never even tried to find me."

"Because Joseph was keeping track of me—and he made sure I knew it."

"What did you think he would do? He didn't want me."

"Exactly. And he would have done his best to turn your . . . Austin against you. That kind of rejection can be devastating to a child or a young woman."

"Was it an easy birth?"

"No, difficult."

"Well, some things don't change. I've been difficult my whole life. Was I on time?"

"Exactly nine months from the date of your conception."

I think I know another reason you wanted to keep me from Joseph Decarlo, Saskia. Are you working up to telling it to me? Or are you hoping I'll figure it out on my own?

"So the photograph appeared in Newsweek . . .*"*

"And my father saw it. Up till then, he had no idea I was living with Kia. I went home before Christmas, stayed a couple of weeks—which didn't please Kia one bit—and gave him a story about working on a ranch outside of Billings, Montana. He approved of that, assumed that eventually I'd come home for good."

I'll have to confirm that with you, Austin. And when I do, maybe then I'll finally know the whole truth.

Sunday

·

SEPTEMBER 24

1:10 P.M.

"Come in, please," Elwood Farmer said.

Nothing had changed here in his small living room since I'd last visited: a fire blazed in the woodstove; his students' pictures adorned the walls; he wore the same plaid wool shirt; it could even have been the same cigarette clamped between his lips.

But, on the other hand, everything had changed.

He motioned for me to sit in one of the padded chairs facing the fire. "I've been expecting you."

"Moccasin telegraph?"

He nodded.

"Then you know I found my mother."

He squinted at me through the smoke from his cigarette, waiting.

"You said something to me when I was here before about familial relationships not being as clear-cut in the Indian world as they are in the white. I've certainly found that to be true. My mother is the great-niece of the woman I thought was my great-grandmother. Which made my adoptive father a cousin at some remove or other. I don't even want to speculate on what my adoptive brothers and sisters are to me."

"Does it matter?"

"A few weeks ago I would have said yes, but now it doesn't. Your nephew Will predicted I'd feel this way. He also said I'd eventually figure out what was more important than my own identity."

"And have you?"

"I'm working on it." I reached into my bag, took out a small gift-wrapped package. "I want to give this to you."

Pleasure spread over his wrinkled face as he took it. I watched him tear the paper and free the silver-framed photograph from it. He studied the picture for a moment, looked questioningly at me.

"I ordered a copy of the original from *Newsweek*'s archives," I told him. "It cost you a great deal to give up the one you had—which I'll always treasure."

He stared down at it, his fingers caressing the silver of the frame, as mine had caressed the buffalo bone.

"I know why it meant so much to you," I added. "Agnes Running Horse thought it was because of Barbara Teton, and I suppose that's partly true. But you also treasured it because of my mother."

He continued to stare at the photograph.

"You could have told me who she was and what she was to you, saved me a lot of running around. And you could have prevented me from involving the DeCarlos."

He looked up, oddly calm and unsurprised. "So you figured it out."

"Yes. Austin was at his father's ranch in California when I was conceived. You were in Fort Hall for the holidays. Kia was upset with Austin for going home. You'd just broken up with Barbara Teton. So you comforted each other."

He set the photograph on the table between us, got up to tend the woodstove. When he sat down again he said, "Well, you have the essence of what happened. I'd gone home to ask Barbara to marry me and come to New York. She refused; instead, she wanted me to come back to the reserve. But I'd moved into a larger world, and there was no returning."

"Why didn't you tell me this before?"

He fished a cigarette from his shirt pocket, contemplated it, then replaced it. "Because until you came here this afternoon I wasn't sure I had a child."

"You must've suspected, though."

"Yes. A number of years ago my cousin Agnes told me Kia was a couple of months pregnant when she ran away with Austin. I sent you to her thinking that Kia might've told her I was the father."

"She didn't."

"Then I suppose Kia either thought you were Austin's child or wanted to believe it."

"She knows exactly whose child I am. She told me I was born nine months *to the day* of my conception. It's not likely she forgot who she was with on that occasion."

The dark, sorrowful current rippled in Elwood's eyes. "But she still didn't tell you about me."

"I think she plans to, but it's hard letting go of a lie you've lived with so long. Austin believed I was his daughter, and on some level the idea of punishing him by putting me up for adoption pleased her. I'm surprised she didn't turn to you, though, after Joseph DeCarlo killed her uncle."

He compressed his lips, stared at the flames flickering behind the glass door of the stove. In a moment he said, "Bad timing."

"What d'you mean?"

"She left a message for me at my rooming house in New York, saying it was an emergency and asking that I call her. But a month earlier, I'd met the woman who later became my wife, and I was spending time at her place. When I finally picked up the message and called, the number turned out to be a phone booth at a truck stop. Kia, of course, was long gone."

"Did you try to locate her?"

"No."

"For God's sake, why not?"

"I was young, in love, and studying hard."

"And there was no room in your life for her."

"That about sums it up."

"What about me? Is there room in your life for me, or do I just go on pretending Austin's my birth father?"

"I've never cared much for pretense."

"Neither have I."

"I've always wanted a child, someone I could pass on the old ways and traditions to."

"I need a father who can help me understand them."

Elwood Farmer stood, lighting a cigarette. "Come back tomorrow," he said.

"What?"

"Tomorrow we'll spend the day together—after we've both had time to assemble our thoughts."

And through the rising smoke, my father winked at me.

Tuesday

·

SEPTEMBER 26

10:10 A.M.

Ma's eyes were sad as I finished telling her the story of the past three weeks. She looked away from me at the flowered wallpaper of her breakfast room, as if its cheeriness offended her.

"I suppose," she said, "you'll be spending a lot of time getting to know your new family now."

"I'm planning to visit Elwood Farmer in November. I want to learn more about the Shoshones."

"And your . . . mother?"

"I'm hoping she'll visit me soon. I like her—her daughter and son too."

Ma sighed. "Life has a strange way of turning out. Andy and I thought adopting you would create an even stronger bond between us, but in the end it created a distance, because of all the lies."

"So why couldn't you tell me this when I first came to you with the petition for adoption?"

"I was afraid. I'd lost Andy—not when he died, but a long time ago, when the lies finally drove him away from all of us. You remember how he was—always hiding in the garage, till he finally slept there nine nights out of ten. I was afraid of losing you, too."

"But by perpetuating those lies, you were guaranteeing you'd lose me."

"Yes, I realize that now. I've finally succeeded in tearing apart what's left of the family." Ma's eyes were bleak as they looked into an empty future.

I tried to understand. Thought of all the nights she'd spent alone when she needed Pa; of all the days, too, when he was withdrawn and depressed. She didn't need any more of that kind of treatment from anyone—including me.

I put my hand on hers where it lay on the table. "Ma, the family's intact. Elwood feels like a father to me, and that's good because I miss Pa a lot. But Kia will be more like a friend or a favorite relative. I already have a mother."

She blinked in surprise, and her mouth twisted. For a moment I thought she might cry, but then the all-too-familiar steely resolve crept into her eyes. I waited. Ma had never been a woman to pass up an opportunity.

"And what of your brothers and sisters? Your nephews and nieces? Jim and Susan? I hope you won't forget them, just because you like this new half sister and brother."

"How on earth *could* I forget them? Even if I wanted to, they wouldn't let me."

Now she smiled. "That's true. They're quite a handful. Always have been. But you were always my good girl—at least as far as I know."

I smiled too. "At least as far as you know, Ma, I'm a very good girl."

Thursday

·

SEPTEMBER 28

7:10 P.M.

"Happy birthday, McCone."

Hy raised his champagne flute to mine, and we clinked softly, then drank. We were seated on the rim of the stone fire pit in our brand-new, mostly unfurnished living room at Touchstone. The sun was a smudge of orange on the horizon, the sea's purple troughs capped by pinkish spray. Gulls, hawks, and ospreys wheeled above, seeking dinner.

He added, "Forty-one tops a banner year for you, huh?"

"Yeah—four new family members. But then there's Austin."

"You break the news to him on the way back from San Diego?"

"I did, and to tell the truth, he seemed relieved. I don't think he's a paternal kind of guy, and he's got enough to handle, after what happened up north. My presence in his life would be one more painful reminder. He said he wants to keep in touch, but I'm betting he won't."

"Is that a loss?"

"No. I never connected with him, and he only thought

he was connecting with me. And then there was his father . . ."

"Some piece of work."

"You know, it's ironic: Joseph DeCarlo committed murder because he thought his son had fathered a child by an Indian woman. Then he spent decades covering up and hating and scheming. He made Austin despise him to the point where he killed him. And in the end it was all so unnecessary."

"Aren't the actions of bigots always unnecessary?"

"Unnecessary, and monstrous."

But it was my birthday; I didn't want to discuss weighty issues. Instead I sampled some pâté that sat along with caviar, Brie, and crackers on the platter between us. "So tell me about your hostage negotiation." He'd tracked me down in Boise on Friday to report it a success.

"Actually, I'm more interested in talking about how we're gonna furnish this place. Comfort is what I care about, so maybe we should—"

The phone rang. I went to where it sat on the floor and answered. John, sounding upset and not bothering to offer me birthday greetings.

"What's wrong?" I asked.

"It's Joey. I finally got news of him, and I don't like it."

"Now what's he done?"

"Ma got a postcard from him this morning. Dated three weeks ago, looked like it'd been misrouted and mangled in the mail. Photo of a place called the Anchor Bay Bar and Grill, said he was working there—"

"Anchor Bay? That's here in the county, south of us."

"I know. Anyway, I called there, talked with the owner. He said Joey didn't show up for his shift a week ago Monday. After a couple of days one of the waitresses—I think she's Joey's girlfriend—went around to the trailer park where he's been living. His truck was gone, so she talked the manager into letting her into the trailer. Everything of his was there, right down to his toothbrush. She's been checking each day, and nothing's changed."

My scalp prickled. "That doesn't sound good."

"No. Shar . . . I know you've been through a lot of heavy-duty family stuff lately, but would you—"

"Go down there and check it out."

"Yeah."

"Let me get my notebook so I can take down the details."

When I replaced the receiver, Hy was standing by the seaward windows watching the last of the sunset. He put his arm around me and drew me close.

"Families!" I said, nestling my head against his shoulder.

"More trouble?"

"Yeah. Why can't humans be hatched from eggs and go our separate ways, like insects?"

He didn't bother to reply. It was a rhetorical question I often voiced, and one to which we both knew the answer. Related or unrelated, we all need each other to get through. Besides, the journey wouldn't be worth much alone.

I watched darkness fall over the sea and thought about the morning. The drive south to Anchor Bay was a pretty one—well worth making if I could find some lead on my missing brother.